"Macca, The Saint and The Screen Goddess" is published by:

Trinity Mirror NW²

Trinity Mirror North West & North Wales
PO Box 48
Old Hall Street
Liverpool L69 3EB

Business Development Director:
Mark Dickinson

Business Development Executive Editor:
Ken Rogers

Written by:
Joe Riley

Design/production:
Zoë Egan, Peter Grant, Emma Smart

Special thanks to the TMNW² Customer Service Team

ISBN 978-1-905266-72-2

In memory of Iris Cawthorne

CONTENTS

READ ALL ABOUT ME

Introduction

Old ones, young ones, even forgotten ones.

Most people may meet a couple of celebrities in their life. I seem to have spent my life surrounded by them.

So I quite surprised myself to rediscover some of the interviews in this particular book.

I am not a microfilm or hard-drive sort of person. It's all in the good old fashioned cuttings.

To date, there are 65 volumes of them, comprising my complete output since joining the Liverpool Echo on January 1, 1974 (after four years on the Daily Post), as what was then the youngest arts editor in the UK.

Although the majority of my journalism has reflected the city's culture over more than three decades, comprising the entire last quarter of the 20th century, I have written on many other subjects. My current brief also includes work as a leader writer and columnist.

So the selection from many millions of words has been a tough call: I have therefore given myself a secondary theme which could be referred to as 'now and then.'

I thought it particularly useful, with hindsight and perspective, to choose a good number of articles about what was once emerging Liverpool talent: folk like Clive Barker and Jonathan Pryce. Not to mention the first interviews with the likes of Willy Russell and Alan Bleasdale.

Then there are those, no longer with us, who are still in need of wider recognition. Arthur Dooley comes readily to mind.

Plus, of course, a goodly dose of nostalgia: talking with Arthur Askey or Leonard Rossiter; or Barbra Streisand filming in Liverpool; the list goes on.

All this then mixed in with some curios - like an encounter with Liverpool sex change April Ashley, or recalling the day I hosted a Saturday afternoon show at the Cavern with Christine Keeler.

Ultimately, there were circumstances which made some tasks unique, such as the last interview given by Quentin Crisp, who died two days before he was due to appear at Liverpool's Unity Theatre. And the Birkenhead woman showing the signs of a stigmata.

A heady mix then from life in Britain's most cosmopolitan and creative city, which explains why I've stayed here all these years, and have no intention of going anywhere else.

Even the earliest articles seem like only yesterday when I re-read them.

It's all been great fun and a great privilege. It still is.

JOE RILEY, September 2008

READ ALL ABOUT HIM

Joe Riley: A foreword by Jean Boht

Joe Riley – arts editor, columnist, leader writer, for more than 34 years at the Liverpool Echo – that's what Google says.

I would add 'extra ordinem' because he just is.

And a nice guy. Statistics tell us that less than 1% of the population is interested in the arts: Joe has none of that and makes you believe it is 99% and 1% have somehow just missed out.

Change 'arts' for 'culture' and he's right.

After all, culture is life itself – entertainment – Anfield and Everton – the pub – theatres and concerts – classical and pop.

I remember first getting to know Joe during those heady years of the big tent on the docks when the Liverpool Philharmonic had to find a home while their hall was being repaired.

Carl Davis, my husband, was made artistic director of the Summer Pops and Philharmonic chief executive Bob Creech together with Joe, myself and Carl looked around for a suitable venue which would hold up to,say, 4,000 concertgoers.

It was finally decided to put up a circus tent on the docks as nowhere else suitable could be found.

The programmes were a mix of classical and popular music with guest artists and programmes for families and children – and what a great time was had by all.

And, of course, Joe was there, often stepping on stage to introduce a show.

Sadly, that all ended in 1999 when the council decided they wanted to do something different and took it over. Now,of course, The Echo Arena has replaced the big tent. So Joe was very much part of that beginning too.

Joe was not around when I began my professional career at the Liverpool Playhouse as a £1 a week student in 1961.

Maud Carpenter was about to retire having been the general manager for 50 years.

Television was just beginning to have an affect on audience attendance and Maud made sure the theatre was as full as it could be.

As a student I was not allowed to be casually dressed outside the theatre, nor were any of the actors.

The males had to wear a suit and girls a hat, gloves and bag and preferably arrive in a taxi at the stage door.

It was legendary that when Maud was invited to see Richard Burton play Hamlet at the Old Vic in London and was asked if she had enjoyed his performance she replied – "Very nice, but the coffee was cold in the interval".

Many years later I came back to Liverpool to film Boys From The Blackstuff in a flat in Sefton Park and then the sitcom Bread, of course, for six weeks filming each year until 1991, and taking up residence as 'twere in Elswick Street. The stage version at the Empire Theatre was its premiere.

Joe looked after us all of course.

So it was great to see him yet again at the opening of the Capital of Culture and as we reminisced and waited to be interviewed by the BBC.

We talked about the Royal Court theatre and the hope the council would accept its responsibility and help in its restoration to enable the National Theatre and the RSC as well as other major touring groups to come to Liverpool as they once used to do in the 60s.

Oh well, Joe, it's always lovely to talk to you, and I am happy to know I can always just ring up and say 'Hello' to a real friend. Carl says he is always grateful to you for all the support you have given over many years to him and the orchestra.

September 2008

Famous fans, Jean
Boht and Carl Davis

A BOY FROM THE BLACKSTUFF

Alan Bleasdale
Writer, Playwright

April, 1976

Alan reminded me that I was the only critic who gave his play Down The Dock Road a good review. He was to become a BAFTA award-winning writer for stage and screen, and one of the country's most respected writers.

THE notice on the door says: "Alan Bleasdale – occasionally…" A joke at Liverpool Playhouse is that their writer in residence doesn't like offices too much and prefers to work at home.

Even so, Bleasdale performs his task conscientiously, writing polite notes to have-a-go playwrights whose scripts he reads, and bashing his own sense of humour out on the typewriter to produce plays for the company.

His latest – his first chance at the big-time of the main auditorium – is about Liverpool's docks.

The 29-year-old former schoolteacher had never been to a theatre voluntarily until he was 20. Now he has a collection of national press cuttings to testify for his competence.

Bleasdale's own background is Roman Catholic working class – "it's surprising how many Liverpool writers are" – and his first love is still Merseyside.

For all that, he resents being called parochial. "Liverpool dialogue is the dialogue I know and can use with strength. But my aim is a universal one, and you've only got to look at characters like Billy Connolly to prove they can go outside a small area and have the widest appeal."

Bleasdale, too, can claim success here. His play, Fat Harold and the Last 26, set in a Merseyside bus depot, went to Colchester and London, and looks set to play Sheffield. (The only changes in the script were the names of some local shops).

And yet to balance out his obvious delight, he calls these outings "a little bit of sugar on the pie."

He always wanted to write for the Playhouse and for Liverpool. This time he's chosen the docks because he knows them, having worked there as a part-time security guard in 1970.

"At first the dockers were very suspicious of me, but when they found I was a school teacher on £17 a week and they were at the time earning around £50 a week, they were very sorry for me and took me under their wing."

"I've tried everything I can to calm down strong language in the play, but at the same time people should realise that a docker doesn't say: 'Dash me, Carruthers!' when something falls on his head."

"What annoys me most of all is that when things get tense in middle class plays, the most outspoken lines can be socially acceptable. But if a working class lad expresses himself in his own limited vocabulary, then everyone gets upset."

"I remember waking up in the middle of the night with a very clear view of the characters I wanted to portray. I made eight or nine pages of notes right there and then."

"What people will see on stage is a very fair reflection of life on the docks, no matter how frightening it may be for some, or how comical for others."

"By frightening I mean that people who are not manual workers will not have an inkling of how important humour and sheer physical skill are to survival."

"I think humour can make a point with far greater effect than by preaching a sermon. I don't like to indoctrinate people. I want them to find their own way through a play."

"The docks play, like all my others, has the more serious message about the past. I firmly believe that we are at present all victims of what has gone before."

And yet he regularly takes stock, and even sends his scripts for a second opinion to his former college lecturer. "All criticism, if it's constructive, is valid," he says.

The Review

FOR Liverpool's 'Mr Scully' it is the big chance. After inventing the incorrigible Scouse schoolboy hero, breaking into television drama and penning two scripts for the Playhouse Studio, Alan Bleasdale, ex-teacher, now confronts a main auditorium audience with his words.

And in keeping with the setting of his latest play, Down the Dock Road, the words are tough, bleak, even crude.

But the way in which Bleasdale works his plan is an honest-to-goodness attempt to lift the lock gates and let a unique breed of humanity make a high-water mark in the city centre, from where it is sadly divorced by the average office worker's ignorance of its soul.

If the turn-round of cargo is up, we cheer; if there are strikes, we howl in protest. However, the headlines in Bleasdale's play are the strident banners of day-to-day team spirit, unifying, dividing and reconciling.

He further refines his ability to observe attitudes as well as turns of phrase, but by serving up a plethora of belly-aching laughter one suspects he has chipped away too much at his more serious intentions.

The real strength lies in wonderful characters like McKenna, the shop steward, Dobbo, Wonderboy and Mastermind.

But the final praise must go to Alan Bleasdale, gradually rooting his style and carving his own niche as a writer.

25.03.1976

Alan Bleasdale (born March 23, 1946) Stage, TV and big screen writer, who still lives in Liverpool.

A FUNNY GIRL ON THE MERSEY

Barbra Streisand
Singer – Actress – Diva

September, 1982

Barbra Streisand, the superstar, came to Liverpool but she kept her distance from the media making her debut as a film director and starring in Yentl. Always making waves in her career – whether as a singer on stage or appearing in another blockbuster – she is the ultimate privacy queen. She was once dubbed an 'official bore'. Funny girl, that Barbra.

BARBRA Streisand had her own day of action yesterday – floating around the River Mersey directing and starring in her latest film. It was action of the 'clapperboard' variety aboard the Manxman, on charter from the Isle Of Man Steam Packet Company.

Now the superstar, known among other things for her theatrical excesses and her false finger nails, is about to depart these shores – as mysteriously as she arrived, safe in the knowledge that her reputation as an unco-operative recluse is untarnished.

Starring in Hello Dolly mid-career, she told Walter Matthau: "I'm not interested in my performance, I want good performances all around me."

Well, in Liverpool that's certainly been the case. Her hoteliers and the shipping company have played their supportive roles well.

Not that the most optimistic of media men expected an interview.

After all, if Streisand once turned down a £50,000 return flight in a privately hired Concorde and half a million dollars for a London concert, what hope was there of her answering a few questions for nothing?

But perhaps the Isle Of Man people could get us on board to do an observational piece? "Sorry, we'd be breaking our contract and we could probably be sued," said a plaintive management voice in Douglas, who would obviously have liked the publicity.

How was Ms Streisand enjoying her stay in a £65 a night top floor suite at the Atlantic Tower Hotel? "Sorry, but we never talk about our guests, even after they've left," said their public relations lady.

As for the Streisand secretary and the Streisand party publicist, they never seemed to be available.

"We didn't even know she was coming here until she turned up on Saturday, although we did know that about 100 other people connected with the filming would be staying here," said the hotel. "She's a very private lady, if a little awkward to people in your profession."

Well, what time does she go out in the morning? "Early."

What time does she return? "That depends on the schedule."

What does she eat for breakfast? "It could be kippers or fried eggs, or even octopus, although that would be difficult, because we don't have octopus!"

It's exactly twelve months to the day since the journalist Donald Zec came to Liverpool to promote his Streisand biography, simply called Barbra, and tried to convince us that Babs was not such a bad girl as the gossip columnists made out.

It would have been nice to meet Funny Girl herself and check it all out.

But that was probably expecting the impossible. For don't the gossip columnists tell us that Ms Streisand now spends her time like a recluse, often completely alone in her Spanish-style Hollywood mansion?

She visits neither clubs nor restaurants, is said to be scared of her fans, and only goes out alone when accompanied by a ferocious dog. By all accounts she isn't even part of the Hollywood establishment. When she was asked to put her footprint for posterity in cement at the Chinese Theatre there she refused.

She's 40 next birthday and perhaps feels that this disassociating herself with the world at large, this rarity of appearance, adds to her charisma?

Was she so aloof, one wonders, when as an already established Broadway star, she promoted her first film, Funny Girl? So many questions, you see, but no answers. Perhaps that's why, by 1970 ,Time Magazine had already placed her in their roll call of "official bores."

The current film, incidentally, is called Yentl and is based on a book by Nobel Prize winner Isaac Bashevis Singer.

The screenplay is by Streisand and Jack Rosenthal and the venture marks Streisand's debut as a director. Since then I've had lunch with her – twice. It's just a cast of getting past her 'minders'.

Barbra Streisand (born New York, April 24, 1942) political activist, film producer and director. She has won Academy Awards for Best Actress and Best Original Song as well as multiple Emmys, Grammys, and Golden Globes.

DRAMA QUEEN'S A REAL TOUCH OF CLASS

Glenda Jackson
Actress

July, 1983

Could she have done a Ronald Reagan (and led her country). A feisty woman with a talent to match. Glenda Jackson, Merseysider, went from stage left to political left. A formidable lady - a formidable talent. And this star of stage and screen certainly got my vote.

WHEN the time comes for Glenda Jackson to retire, she'll do it graciously.

There won't be any of the neuroses or the sad hanging on, that has characterised the twilight years of many another stage career.

There again, at 47, Miss Jackson is not about to qualify for slippers and a theatrical goodnight kiss: it's just that the theatre itself is not very kind to women of her age.

"The work is not there for women of my mature years," she says, allowing the angle-iron features to bend themselves in to a smirk.

"And one thing's certain. I'm not going to hang around to play the nurse in Romeo and Juliet. Nor am I going to spend all day polishing furniture."

But there are other things than theatre. What about television? Directing? Writing? What about more film work?

"I don't know whether I've abandoned television or whether television has abandoned me, because I have always been so rude about it. I don't find it an interesting media to act in at all," says the former Elizabeth R.

"I'm too bossy to be a director and couldn't be a producer: I can just about add up the bills at the supermarket checkout.

"As for writing, I can't even manage a postcard. Admittedly some people have offered to write parts for me, but I've always warned them against it, because it usually means they want you to repeat something, some kind of thing that you've already done."

Glenda Jackson was, of course, an immediate success in the film world: major roles have included Ken Russell's Women in Love and The Music Lovers; John Schlesinger's Sunday, Bloody Sunday and most of her other works – Mary, Queen of Scots, Bequest to Nation, and A Touch of Class, for which she received her second Academy Award.

But even that track record doesn't fight off the falls of the business, and she says that a film called Buried Alive, in which she was to have starred with Dirk Bogarde, has had to be abandoned because they can't raise the money.

"My mum has polished all my awards down to the base, but I wouldn't want her to come to the plays. It would put me off that vital suspension of reality for the part, if I thought she was thinking "that's our Glen up there." Besides, she'd fall asleep."

If she escaped from it all, what would she do? "I wouldn't mind getting myself a higher education. I left school in West Kirby with three school certificates as they were called then – in English language, English literature and geography."

"If I went back to college then they'd have to plead a special case for me and I could go in as a mature student."

Failing that, her other choice would probably be work for Voluntary Service Overseas.

She could even turn to politics. After all her life-long support of the Labour Party is an open secret. That loyalty remains, despite the party splits.

"I no longer know whether I'm left of centre or centre centre."

Her words about Thatcher are even more scathing: "How Jimmy Tarbuck and Kenny Everett, both good Liverpool lads, could get up on that platform, I don't know," she says.

She's also proud that she got a letter to ask if she'd like to fight Winston Churchill in the last General Election.

"I told them that if they nursed me for five years then I'd have a go."

Glenda May Jackson, CBE, (born Wirral, May 9, 1936) British actress and politician, currently Labour Member of Parliament for Hampstead and Highgate in the London Borough of Camden.

THE MINISTER, THE MODEL AND THE RUSSIAN SPY

Christine Keeler
Model and Headline Maker

August ,1989

Christine Keeler gave new meaning to the phrase 'femme fatale' when she was a central figure in the Profumo scandal which brought down the Conservative government of the 60s. I met her in the Cavern and found her to be politically correct.

WHEN Ms Christine Keeler walked into the Cavern – a collision of 60s phenomena if ever there was – a friend suggested she may be carrying a tan leather bag full of knitting.

A generation on, Christine, who actually broke into the news under the banner headline: The minister, the model and the Russian Spy (in which she played the part of the model), may have been transformed into a quiet, suburban heap of anonymity.

Not quite. She materialised in a polka dot frock, still slim, trim and full of vim.

So where had she been this last quarter century, since the political world from Moscow to Washington had been rocked to the foundations by her very fibre?

"Oh, trying to be ordinary", she says. "I married a couple of times, but always on the rebound."

The main concern in her life now is her 17-year old son, at college in the south, and by all accounts missing mum.

Meanwhile, Ms Keeler, an even more famous housewife superstar in her day than Dame Edna Everage, is touring the country promoting her book and somebody else's film.

"We have had our ups and downs with these film people", she told me, unleashing a fear that the entire interview may now be a shuffling of innuendo.

Both movie and tome are called Scandal.

But the book has the edge, as here, the title is followed by an exclamation mark (!), as well it may be…

"The film covers people very well. In that sense, they've made it into a people's film. But you need to read my book to realise what people did behind the scenes."

Point taken. I hadn't even reached puberty when I was first forced to ask my parents what was meant by a 'two-way mirror' and why they had already had one at a place called Wimpole Mews.

Ms Keeler was not only behind the scenes, but in many of the ones which made up that sexually and politically cosmic experience known as the Profumo Affair.

The stuff of both novels and navels. It's not every Saturday I spend the afternoon chatting about espionage, with names like Macmillan and Kennedy interwoven with talk of Cuban missiles, secret cameras beneath the waters of the English Channel and rats gnawing away at nuclear warheads.

But what could be said that had not been said?

Christine says that the nasty tabloid nationals have been making things up about her. Writing words she never spoke. "I was used as a scapegoat as a 19-year-old kid, and some people are still trying."

She has been setting the record straight for more than 20 years. She began her book back in 1968, worked it through three drafts, and now produces it in self defence. "You can put in a book what you can't get into a film", she insists.

Her 'chat' is heavily laiden, most pointedly about Dr Stephen Ward, described at the time as a society osteopath. Well wasn't he?

"Oh I suppose he had about two patients, but it was a cover-up. Even the film leaves out the fact that Stephen was spying. I knew it anyway, which is why I betrayed him.

"In 1962 he tried to make a meeting between the Russians and the Americans. By this time, missiles were already on their way to Cuba.

"He did it for money… he was a very clever man."

"John Profumo (the then Minister of War, who had a liaison with Ms Keeler) did not resign because he lied (to the House of Commons). He resigned because Stephen had to be got.

"Earlier, MI5 didn't know that Stephen had information, nor did the press, nor did the government."

She says that at the time she met Profumo, she had a Persian boyfriend. But she met so many people.

"I am not a pretentious person. I have no ego. I have written this for the sake of our history, really."

She will, however, be virtually circumnavigating the globe, as once again her life is put under the microscope.

But this is not likely to happen in places like Italy and France, where they still can't understand what all the fuss was about back in '63.

A scandal? Surely just a chapter in the life of a red-blooded male called Jack the Lad.

Undoubtedly, shades of the historian, Thomas Macaulay, writing a full century earlier in the Edinburgh Review: "We know no spectacle so ridiculous as the British public in one of its periodic fits of morality."

And as Ms Keeler had just stepped off the train from Edinburgh, and would soon to be on her way back to London, there's another apt old story worth a meal ticket.

Christine Keeler (born February 22, 1942) model and showgirl. Her involvement with a British government minister discredited the Conservative government of Harold Macmillan in 1963, in what is known as the Profumo Affair.

SPEAKING WORDS OF WISDOM

Norman Wisdom
Comedian, Film Star

September, 1989

**Norman Wisdom was a multi-talented performer I had
always admired. So I enjoyed being in the audience
watching this unique clown in action.**

ONE of my ambitions when I took this job was to see all of the
great acts live on stage before TV technology took such a grip
that the art of "working an audience" would depend on how
many re-takes could be afforded.

One man who knows all about timing, whether he is rolling on
the floor or sitting behind a drum kit, is the incredible Mr Norman Wisdom.

Norman, now rumoured to be in his early 70s (not even Who's
Who records his date of birth) is still a cult figure – among the
young.

Is it because he is young in heart, or simply because even a
new generation is becoming disenchanted with plastic stereo-
types?

For Wisdom does it all: sings, tells jokes, throws his torso from
one side of the stage to the other, and then plays a host of instruments. Last night's show included solos on trumpet, piano, sax-

ophone, clarinet and even hunting horn.

The drums were incorporated into the sort of knockabout slap-stick routine that used to be reserved for the silent movies.

So did the tripping, falling over, and apparently forgetful clum-siness, which go toward making Wisdom the sort of natural clown for which there seems to be no mould left.

I did notice, for the first time, how this time-served practitioner has influenced Michael Crawford, one of the few artists who has brought the old stage crafts through into the New Age.

It is not just the physicality. Even the little boy-lost expressions and the voice show a remarkable similarity.

Believe it or not, Wisdom still looks quite boyish: a full head of hair, a cheek-to-cheek grin, and the agility of someone more than half his years.

To be able to look at a stage and say: "Eeh, son, that's Norman Wisdom you're seeing out there" is the stuff of legend.

What's more, this master of slapstick still does a six-day week, five of them twice-nightly, as they used to call it in the great days of variety.

I was not so impressed with supporting act Pink Champagne. They come from Tinsel and Glitter Land, and their hour-long music/comedy/dance routine is brimming over with mediocre antics.

In short, the sort of stuff which is filling our theatres nowadays like quick-setting cement.

Sir Norman Wisdom, OBE (born, London, February 4, 1915) is an English comedian, singer and actor.

A HAPPY ROYAL APPOINTMENT

The Prince & Princess of Wales

December, 1982

Prince Charles and Princess Diana came to Liverpool.

IT IS the season of goodwill and fairytale magic – and for a congregation of over 2000 in Liverpool Cathedral last night both elements rang true as a future king brought his princess to a Christmas celebration in words and music.

The Prince and Princess of Wales were visibly moved by the splendour and spectacle.

With television cameras focused on them, children from St. Winifred's School, Toxteth, enacted a nativity scene at the end of the ceremony, and presented the princess with a toy lamb for Prince William.

Despite the assembled throng, the royal couple were determined that they should be able to join in a private act of worship, the proceeds from which, via ticket money and donations, were going to aid the Prince's Trust.

Yes, there were happy times - and this seemed to be one of them. The prince and Princess spent half an hour at a private reception where they chatted with 50 Merseyside young people.

But once they entered the Nave by a side staircase from the reception rooms, it was a case of fanfares, organ music and full-blooded congregational singing.

Like Pope John Paul II, who made the same long walk beneath

the world's highest Gothic arches in the summer, they were noticeably impressed by the ethereal pomp and circumstance of it all – and by the warmth of feeling.

When the Bishop of Liverpool, the Rt. Rev David Sheppard, asked for a "traditional Merseyside welcome" the congregation clapped long and loud.

The prince read the first lesson – the story of the angels appearing to the shepherds – but the mainstay of the celebration was the music, with a solo from head chorister Geoffrey Williams and the performance of a new carol written by assistant organist Ian Wells.

"It was marvellous. The acoustics are really tremendous," the prince told local dignitaries before he and the princess became the first royals to leave the cathedral by the Great West Doors.

The doors were not finished when the Queen came to the cathedral's official completion ceremony in 1978.

And in departing in such way a way, Prince Charles completed a Royal sequence of events – literally at either end of the cathedral's history.

For his great-great grandfather, Edward VII, laid the foundation stone in 1904; his great-grandfather, George V, attended the consecration 20 years later; his grandfather , George VI, visited during the war and urged the continuation of building work despite the blitz; and his mother has been there three times: first for the inauguration of the bells in 1951, then during her jubilee year, in 1978.

The couple separated in 1993. Diana spoke publicly about her problems and her own and her husband's infidelities in a TV film in November 1995. The marriage formally ended with a decree absolute in August 1996. Diana was killed in a car crash in 1997.

Prince Charles and Camilla Parker-Bowles married on April 9 2005.

POSH SCOUSE – AS SURE AS EGGS IS EGGS

Edwina Currie
Politician turned author and celebrity

April, 1999

Nobody mentions eggs as Edwina Currie scans the menu at a cosy London eaterie.

"SHALL we order our dinner?" she asks.

It is lunchtime, but I know what she means. That's what they used to call midday nibbles in post war Wavertree, and these things stick – as do headlines.

Incredibly, it's 10 years since Edwina blurted on red alert about the perils of salmonella in the nation's egg supply and ended up with more fractures than Humpty Dumpty.

A plate of garnished tomatoes will suffice plus ordinary tap water. "I hate that stuff" she tells a waiter brandishing a bottled alternative.

Edwina is sunny side up, a strikingly highlighted hairdo topping out a demo in deportment which makes her look strangely like spare parts for the queen. In the age of the Spice Girl, definitely Posh Scouse.

A decade on from breaking eggs with a big stick, this daughter of a Williamson Square tailor is out of government, out of Parliament, but well into her new love of being the wireless hostess with the most-ess.

Late Night Currie – Radio 5, Saturdays, Sundays,10pm-1am reaches half a million listeners and takes 1,000 calls a night: "It helps that people think they know me. I'm always Edwina and if people want to argue, they're free to do so. They also know that, occasionally, I'll come back and bite their nose off."

There's even a new slot nick-named ER – Edwina's Rant.

That's nothing new. I'm chewing fat with the lady who hectored northerners for their bad diets, told old folk to wrap up more in the winter, smokers to bite their nails and businessmen to take their wives abroad on work trips.

That afternoon, she was collecting a new car. "A Hyundai, coupé style. I like a car I can find in the car park. I don't like saloon cars." And a bargain by all accounts: "It cost less than the car I'm trading in cost four years ago."

Edwina is revving up, reflecting on her new persona as member of – rather than punch bag for – the media.

"My image is of an aggressive and loudmouthed person, but I confound that by being chillingly polite. I have power when I'm on the air and it's not for me to abuse that by grinding someone's face into the dust. Anyway, the best way of putting someone down is to be witty."

Radio hates silences, she reminds me. But what chance of that? On Saturday nights, she delights that soccer fans returning home in their coaches are shouting at her. The switchboard gets jammed. The mobile phone has come into its own: lorry drivers have good ones. The best is a milkman who phones in regularly.

But so do teachers, doctors, police officers, lawyers and even judges. That's your Sunday audience but too often male led.

"Five Live was known as Radio Bloke when it started. But when the girls think it's not their programme, I shout at them, " says Edwina, who goes on to demonstrate machismo.

"I do hard news, and the issues are getting harder all the time… we are the only such BBC programme live at that period, so whatever the issues are, we get them. We can commandeer studios all over the country and we do. We take precedence".

The Drumcree marches, the Omagh bombing, the riots in Marsailles, the Bulger case, Stephen Lawrence, the bombing of Yugoslavia. The entire world's Edwina's stage: "It's helpful to have had a hugely diverse background in politics. It's rare to come across an issue I haven't dealt with".

What a wonder doing two weeks of stand-ins for Jimmy Young on Radio 2 can do for your future radio philosophy:

"I sometimes feel myself holding a ball of light and seeing where the rays go into the darkened corners. And I can carry that ball of light as the leader of the discussion."

When the FM stations linked in with her programme last September, Radio Merseyside's audience suddenly found themselves with a portion of Currie: "This chap from Liverpool had a tirade against Tory MPs taking jobs with the BBC. Thanks to him, I came up with my trademark comment 'I've had the operation', I'm no longer an MP".

But Edwina can still be political. Isn't the Tory Party finished, I asked, adding that it certainly is in Liverpool? "When it comes to public pronouncements I am cautious because I may want to interview these people", she counters. But then adds with vigour: "We have the greatest difficulty in persuading Tories that it is worth giving up half an hour on a Saturday to be on mainstream BBC.

"This is ridiculous when William Hague is telling senior members they must learn from past mistakes. Everybody else is too busy talking to each other. The media is seen as a bit of a nuisance."

An exception is Archie Norman, the Tory vice chairman, who pops up from nowhere, and now seems to be numbered with other Edwina life influencing saints such as Sir Keith Joseph and Harold Macmillan, whom she first heard extolling the virtues of the European Community at Liverpool's Philharmonic Hall in January '63.

Edwina was schooled at nearby Blackburne House: "I remember thinking if I agree with him then I must be a Tory. We had debates at school on the big issues of the day. I took the pro-European side, lost, but convinced myself."

But she was disenchanted with Liverpool at the time: "A whole generation of us – sixth formers at the main school – decided that unless you wanted to work for Littlewoods or the Royal Insurance, there was nothing there for us".

Edwina Currie went on to 22 years in public life mainly as a councillor in Birmingham and later as a much publicised junior Health Minister at Westminster.

Any chance of a return to politics?

"I'm 53 next birthday. If I were to try and get back into Parliament, I would almost certainly be spending some of the best years of my life in Opposition and Opposition back bench is not a fun place to be. I've been in the ring slogging it out, and not just at the ringside... if I'd wanted a pleasant experience right through life, I'd have done gardening."

Ex MPs, she assures me, do a good job of keeping in touch "depending which conspiracy they consider themselves to be of" and some of what she calls the residual exasperation with politics is found in her novels together with lots of fun (although Auberon Waugh gave her a prize for writing the worst sex scene).

Of the still living Blair, she says: "He's done two things extremely well: worked out what made his party unelectable and ditched the lot, and then what made the Tories electable. In those circumstances any Opposition is on a hiding to nothing."

Edwina Currie Jones née Cohen, (born Liverpool October 13, 1946) is a former Conservative MP from 1983 to 1997 including three years as Junior Health Minister, before resigning in 1988 because of a controversy over salmonella in eggs.

READ ALL ABOUT HIM... ER... HER

April Ashley
Model, Author

April, 1982

April Ashley made the news as Merseyside's most famous transsexual. I met this extraordinary person at her home in Hay-on-Wye.

A BRAVE woman. Nowadays everyone's being snipped in search of their true identity. But in those days you risked a lynch mob.

From caterpillar to chrysalis to butterfly: that's the story of Liverpool-born George Jamieson, who became Toni April and is now April Ashley, once billed in a London show as The Most Talked about Woman in the World.

Now she is ready for the off. "I can pack a case faster than anyone I know." She's just come back from America and it looks like she'll jet her way to Australia, possibly for an extended stay.

Hay-on-Wye, where April lives in a rambling red-brick house she inherited from an old man called Charlie, is the last place you'd expect to find a compulsive traveller.

But she came here to get away from the social roller-coasting of the big cities, to get over an unpleasant conclusion to a restaurant business she once partly owned and to repair her health.

Today after two heart attacks (and three youthful suicide attempts) she's still with us, not afraid to turn a marvellously grand sense of humour against herself at times, but still wanting a new challenge.

"I'm 47, but I still feel sixteen. Okay, sometimes I look in the mirror in the morning and say 'Darling, you look great' and other mornings I look like an old dog, and count the chins."

Such frank admissions come easily, like the one that she's a stone overweight – or so she reckons.

"After all, when you've been medically examined from head to foot and the evidence given in open court, you learn not to be embarrassed," she says.

The court case resulted in the annulment of her marriage to the honourable Arthur Cameron Corbett whose family money came from Brown and Poulson's cornflour.

The hearing turned into a medical jamboree. "They even X-rayed my hands to show that certain bones hadn't fused together at puberty. So technically, I never reached puberty."

April was conceived in the Isle of Man and born in Smithdown Road Hospital on April 29th, 1935.

From the apparent evidence, her Protestant mother Ada, and her Catholic father, Fred, christened the baby George.

At first they lived in Pitt Street and then moved to a council estate in Norris Green. A house in Teynham Crescent became home, but, as April recalls "Since the rest of Pitt Street moved with us, along with the equally notorious Scotland Road, the atmosphere continued to be full of fists."

George was a puny child. At the age of 15, he still looked no more than eleven. His sole companion was a mongrel pointer dog called Prince, who would wait outside while he watched The Perils of Pauline at the Broadway Regal.

After he left school, the distraught George would frequent the gays bars, where he would see some men in drag. They were transvestites, and George could neither identify with them or the homosexuals.

He wanted TO BE a woman.

At eighteen he felt there was no chance of happiness, so he jumped in the Mersey thinking "thank God the tide wasn't out".

The current carried him off at top speed and he seemed to be going towards New Brighton, when, all of a sudden – yank…

Somebody had come to the rescue: "The ECHO gave me my first press. The headline said: "Youth saved by long hair."

But as time went on, April Ashley was to be in the headlines as much as the Queen or Jackie Kennedy. She became the sex change cause celebre, but why?

"When the story broke, I was a top model, I was extremely beautiful, and if I went for audition with two hundred other ravishing beauties, I could still beat them. Now there must be something special about that. I mean some men could have sex changes, but they'd still look like dockers in dresses. I was different."

When I first saw her, out shopping in the narrow streets of Hay with sunglasses, white slacks and a lavender-coloured top, she cut the sort of figure that demands attention, irrespective of who she is.

But once at the house, she insisted on changing: "I must just go and slip into a frock and look nice for the photographer…"

Following her everywhere is a whippet called Flora Bella, "so named because she was born on the floor".

At present there is no-one special in April's life although there have been. People like Joey, a cockney with Italian and Irish blood.

And then there was Edward, a drama student, killed in a car accident near Paris.

But in Hay, April Ashley lives alone. If friends call to see her she'll go to the pub where the lady behind the bar says she's now accepted as one of the locals.

"Of course, once the tourist season starts and people find out who I am, then they'll always stare. You're suddenly aware of faces turning in your direction. And I still get kids calling after me. I usually ignore it but once in a while, I'll turn around and give them what for.

"But I've got a good amount of Liverpudlian commonsense and my humour doesn't desert me when I need it."

April Ashley (born George Jamieson on April 25, 1935) is an English model and restaurant hostess. She was famously outed as a transsexual by the British press in 1961.

KING ARTHUR – THE BUSIEST BEE

Arthur Askey
Comedian

June, 1980

Small of stature, big-hearted Arthur was a great local hero and one of Ken Dodd's inspirational predecessors. I met him for his 80th birthday celebrations. A much-missed man.

ARTHUR Askey is 80 on Friday – yet still as busy as the bee in that comic song that has become one of the hallmarks of his career.

The diddyman born in the front bedroom of 29 Moses Street, Dingle, on June 6, 1900, now lives in a plush fifth floor flat off London's Kensington High Street, surrounded by the memorabilia of more than 50 years in show business.

There's even the music cabinet he received before it all started – back in 1923, as a leaving present from colleagues in Liverpool Education Offices, many of whom thought he was mad to forsake security for the hit or miss life of the theatrical.

The music cabinet, like the grand piano and sideboard, are covered in attractive Chinese lacquer work, decorative additions commissioned by his wife, May, who died six years ago.

Arthur now lives with his sister, Rene, who never married.

"She looks after me marvellously, she's a wonderful cook and an excellent shorthand typist into the bargain," says the man himself, beaming with a kind of smile that introduces one ear to another.

Arthur Askey was born at the tidy end of show business, before it became fashionable to look avante garde, or, if you prefer, a mess. He sports an immaculate tiger-tooth check suit, blue shirt and tie, and comfortable casual shoes.

He appears as sprightly as ever, but as he later admits, he's now having to use a stick from time to time following two falls.

"It's only by the grace of God that I'm 80," says Arthur, who has beaten two heart attacks. "It's not an achievement. I mean, I was with Stanley Holloway the other day and he's in his 90th year, so there a few ahead of me. He's going a little deaf, but by gum, that resonance is still there in his voice and he's still got that lovely laugh."

The phone rings, somebody wants to know if Arthur will take part in special discussions about the early years of radio. He provisionally agrees and says he will check his diary and let him know.

"I imagine I'm news again. I've recorded a religious programme for the Songs of Praise spot. I suppose I got asked because I was a choirboy back at St. Michael's in the Hamlet in Liverpool and then sang the first solo in Liverpool Cathedral when the Lady Chapel was consecrated in 1911."

Arthur is a man with few regrets, but one, undoubtedly is that nobody invited him to the cathedral completion service two years ago, which was an all-ticket affair. "I'm the last to write cap-in-hand, but not to worry, it was rather a long time ago. I'm a very private person really. I dodge all the hospitality rooms after the shows. That's probably why I have lasted as long as I have. Yet I still get a kick out of it, although I've got to watch things a little bit now. I even take my stick on stage with me when I get lots of sympathy. I still do the Bee-Song complete with actions, but I do it slower and get a big 'aagh."

That incredible song has buzzed itself through so much of Arthur Askey's career and still managed to bring the house down when he was last in Liverpool three years ago in a charity show at the Empire attended by Prince Charles. It was, in fact, written by another Liverpool comedian called Kenneth Blain.

Arthur paid his two guineas for the rights to sing it in a summer show at Shanklin and later paid another two guineas to use it in his London performances.

Then one day, Arthur was stuck for a song in his famous Band Wagon radio show and he included the Bee, which hitherto he had kept for his stage act. It has stuck with him ever since; he has recorded it three times, and it even made the number one spot in the 30s. Those were the days when Arthur was Britain's number one showbiz name. But for May Askey, nee Swash, the girl he had met when she was a typist at Goodlass Wall, the paint manufacturers in Liverpool, and who had later taken part in his concert party shows under the name of May Bowden, the adulation and the publicity were not a welcome thing.

"In a more serious mood, I think my success may rather have hastened my wife's end. I mean that. She was basically a very, very shy woman. She wouldn't even bother to go to the Palladium to see me in a Royal Command show. I'd come home and say it had gone well and she'd merely say 'Oh good', and go on to tell me how lucky she'd been to get the last brown loaf at Harrods that afternoon."

"Even as early as 1938 when I came to prominence with Band Wagon I remember our family doctor telling me that he didn't think May could take my success, and he was right. Our daughter, Anthea, was at boarding school. I was on tour and she would be on her own for a long time. She was not a good mixer. We lived in blocks of flats for most of our lives, but she wouldn't know the lady next door."

But for his mother Betsy, it was a different story. Arthur reckons that his success added years to her life. She was a great royalist and the walls of the front parlour were covered in pictures of the royal family. But when Arthur rose to stardom the royals came down and he went up.

Today, her son is known and loved by the royal family. King George V was a great fan of Band Wagon, as he used to tell his cabinet ministers. In his career Arthur had done 12 command shows.

His own flat is covered with pictures of what he terms "Yer royals," but this time he's standing next to them.

Arthur Askey CBE (born Liverpool June 6, 1900 – died November 16, 1982).

FROM HUYTON TO HOLLYWOOD

Rex Harrison
Actor

February, 1983

They used to call him sexy Rexie. He was the immaculate English actor of the black-tie tradition. The fair sex were beguiled by the flair and the style.

TODAY in his 75th year, he can no longer claim to be a sex symbol – although he is enjoying his sixth marriage. Mercia Tinker is an independently wealthy lady who is three decades his junior.

But the style, now tweedy, is still there, and when I met him he was sporting his first set of real whiskers.

"When I did Henry VIII on Broadway, I simply stuck the beard on. I thought that this time we'd have the real thing," he said.

Harrison is back on the British stage for the first time in six years, playing a vigorous 88-year-old in Bernard Shaw's Heartbreak House.

What's more, he looks every bit as distinguished as Shaw, to whom he owes the main-stay of his career; after all, My Fair Lady, in which he played Professor Higgins in New York, London and on film, is a product of Pygmalion.

Rex Harrison was a lad of five, living in Lancaster Avenue, Sefton Park, when Shaw wrote Pygmalion in 1913.

He then went to Liverpool College, where he admits to having been "hugely unsuccessful," and then on to Liverpool Playhouse, where as a 16-year-old he got a studentship, doing everything from brushing the stage to bit parts, and earning 30 shillings a week.

His first appearance was as the husband in something called Thirty Minutes in a Street.

His last appearance in his home city - he was born in Tarbock Road, Huyton – was 12 years ago.

"I used to like coming back, but I have no relatives here now."

Indeed, Harrison admits to being a man without a proper home. He's sold his house at Cap Ferrat, on the French Mediterranean coast, and his place at Portofino in Italy.

"We have a small two-roomed apartment in New York, but that's all," he says, adding that he hasn't ruled out the possibility of returning to the English countryside.

But he has no plans for retirement.

"If I like something then I'll do it. If not, I certainly won't."

As a millionaire, you can be that choosey. Way back in '49 he was pulling in £54,000 a year, ahead of folk like Bing Crosby, Bob Hope, Tyrone Power and Edward G. Robinson in the Hollywood earnings league.

Quite apart from his Oscar, and all the other accolades which the entertainment industry has showered upon him, his private life has always been in the headlines.

The other Mrs. Harrisons were Marjorie Thomas, Lilly Palmer, Kay Kendall (who died of leukaemia), Rachel Roberts and Elizabeth Harris, the ex-wife of Richard Harris.

But he's been wed to Mercia, a one-time neighbour in Monte Carlo, for the past five years.

One of his first Liverpool memories is being taken to the old Royal Court to see Fred Terry and Julian Neilson in The Scarlet Pimpernel.

After leaving the Playhouse in 1927 to appear in a London production of Charley's Aunt, his career really took off. Since then it's never really come in to land.

In all those years he's bumped into the great and famous, including Bernard Shaw himself –"very strong and very opinionated, but with a marvellous sense of humour".

And Noel Coward — "a very difficult man to follow in his own plays because he wrote them for himself."

But today Rex Harrison, thanks to the new beard, enjoys walking round the streets unnoticed and indulging in his new hobby, painting.

"They're mainly water colours of landscapes and seascapes.

I must try portraits sometime," he said.

"It's all come about because I travel around so much. I particularly like to paint out of doors."

Sir Reginald "Rex" Carey Harrison (born Huyton, Liverpool 5 March 1908 died June 2, 1990). Academy Award and Tony Award-winning theatre and film actor.

DOOLEY'S DESIGNS FOR PEACE

Arthur Dooley
Sculptor

April, 1982

One of my own favourite cultural tsars. Came to Liverpool's Pilgrim Poets group as a guest and read St. Paul's "faith, hope and charity" epistle from a great illuminated bible. Not a dry eye in the house.

ARTHUR Dooley – sculptor. He's been doing it now for 25 years and there was a time, during the late 60s Liverpool do-it-yourself art boom, when he was on the telly with the frequency of Michael Parkinson.

Now he's 54, has worked for the past two years in a vast indoor scrapyard of a place on a Liverpool industrial estate and has just written an open letter to the Pope.

What's more, the incoming mail has included a leaf of Buckingham Palace headed notepaper, saying that his message to the Pope has been "laid before Her Majesty." That's because he sent her a copy.

Basically, he's telling the Pontiff that his visit to England will be "a waste of time" unless he will go on record as saying that the Protestant churches are divinely inspired and that their ministers are properly ordained, and always have been.

Is the sculptor turning into a theologian? Not at all, he would argue. Just speaking out to end 500 years of bloody wars, slaughters and martyrdoms in the name of Jesus Christ.

And why not? Dooley was born a Protestant but converted to Roman Catholicism 35 years ago. Today he attends churches of both denominations.

What's more, his first sculpture was a crucifix, although he still says his largest was fitting flanges to a bulk-head on the Ark Royal when he was a 14 year old apprentice at Cammell Laird's.

Yes, he did go to art school, when he worked as a janitor watching how things were done.

But his training, he says, was "more medieval, Byzantine almost," by which he means damned hard work.

"I've never stopped working hard. It's nothing to work here from eight in the morning until ten at night." After which he cycles home to Dingle.

On the way he passes near to his Black Christ statue in Princes Road.

"That's what exhibiting means. Having your work properly before the public,.

Failing that, there's the telly. "With a million viewers, who needs art galleries?"

Not for Arthur the clique thing of first nights, sipping glasses of sherry and sounding intense.

"One thing they don't learn at art school is how to sell work. Today I do it by word-of-mouth but I don't give people delivery dates, I give them seasons. Next spring, I say."

And so the Dooley following has grown, until there are now more than 2,000 pieces in places like civic halls, museums, libraries and private homes.

The stuff's not cheap either. A three foot high figure fully cast in metal could knock you back £600.

The only typical thing about Arthur Dooley is the varying time he needs, according to that much over-used word 'inspiration.'

"You can sit and think for six hours or six days before the penny drops. Even then, I've known myself to work for months on a job and then scrap it."

But inspiration, when it comes, is most often on religious themes. Indeed, most of those 2,000 or so works, are in, or near churches.

Which brings us back to the Pope's visit and the fact that Dooley has put his money where his mouth is.

He's donating a crucifixion scene to the Metropolitan Cathedral for the chapel of St. Paul of the Cross. He also wants to give an Amnesty International figure to the Anglican Cathedral.

But the greatest joy of his life is his independence.

Forty per cent of the nation, he says, is breast-fed by the state, although he has a rather more colourful way of telling you over a cup of tea.

That goes, he says, for the students on their grants, the folk on the social, and those employed by the state.

Arthur's his own man, and a moderate man at that. When it comes to religion, he seems well capable of seeing all points of view.

"I think the Orange Lodge are also part of the mystical body of Christ. They have a point to make and they should be listened to like everyone else."

That, coming from a man with a calendar of the Pope and a picture of the Shroud of Turin on the wall above his workbench.

"I remember being told by a Catholic priest that the Reformation should have happened, but it should have happened within the church. Now I want the Pope to embrace the Reformation and say it was divinely inspired.

"Indeed, the Catholic Church needs its own reformation or it will be left like a stranded whale on the beach gasping for air."

"The Catholic Church should be part of the Protestant church. I don't think it will happen next week, but time is running out."

As a specific instance of reform, he believes that priests or nuns should be allowed to marry if they fall in love. "A lot of vocations are being lost because of this ruling, and as far as I can see, there's nothing in the Bible to forbid it."

Standing there in this blue boiler suit, training shoes and woollen hat, speaking in an attempt to build those bridges between the faiths, Arthur also tells you that when it comes to metal work, he could build you a real bridge if you asked for one. Or a pair of earrings.

Which is probably why he doesn't seem immodest when he says he's the "best in the world at what I do."

He's had two holidays in the past 15 years: one to Butlins and one to Spain.

His idea of a good night out is good company and a good meal. Certainly at Arthur's table, the conversation would never flag.

Arthur Dooley born Liverpool 1929 - died 1994. There are plans to open a permanent display of his sculpture studio in his home town.

49

RIGSBY MEETS SCROOGE

Leonard Rossiter
Actor

December, 1975

Leonard Rossiter was a great guy! The actor used to like visiting the Liverpool Echo and seeing the sub-editors producing the pages. He told me he would have loved to have been a journalist.

LEONARD Rossiter has grown used to people asking him for digs. It's the most well-worn quip in the book since he became the nation's number one landlord in television's Rising Damp comedy series.

"Dare I say it, but I think the series would work just as well with a lesser cast," says Liverpool-born Rossiter.

"By that, I mean that the scripts are so rich in imagery that people can hardly fail to identify with them. The material is there on paper."

On the other hand, he never wants to over-identify with a role. That's why he's said 'no' at present to another series of Rising Damp.

"I think it's time to do something else."

It's also the reason he told the BBC. that three months as Inspector Bamber in the 1960s Z Cars would be long enough.

It's surprising that he stuck a desk job for more than seven years.

"I joined the Commercial Union claims department in Liverpool and worked in that big white building.

"At that time I was quite heavily involved in amateur dramatics on Merseyside with the East Wavertree Players, The Green Room, Wavertree Community Centre Players and a company at Speke called Ad Astra."

Originally, Rossiter had intended reading modern languages at university after leaving Liverpool Collegiate.

Today he's a little unhappy over what the planners have done to the old town.

"Seeing that development around the Royal Court makes me feel a bit depressed."

Apart from his visit to the Court with A Christmas Carol, Liverpool audiences haven't seen much of Leonard.

"It's quite amazing really.I did the musical Free As Air at the Court in 1958 and The Ice Man Cometh at the Shakespeare around the same time, but that's all."

Leonard Rossiter (born Liverpool October 21, 1926 – died October 5, 1984).Best known for his roles as Rupert Rigsby in the British comedy television series Rising Damp and as the eponymous Reginald Perrin.

BEATLES SACKED – WORLD EXCLUSIVE

Allan Williams
Impresario

February, 1999

**The man who told the Beatles they'd never work again.
He must pinch himself every day and say: 'If only...**

ALLAN Williams says the time has come to rewrite history.

He is not, as the title of his autobiography suggests, The Man
Who Gave The Beatles Away – "I sacked them," he insists.

There follows a gurgling chuckle like a sink emptying. Has life
gone down the plughole for the Fab Four's first manager?

Not at all.

He travels the world telling tales of how it was – and how it
might have been. The past 12 months have seen him in Mexico,
the Dominican Republic, Cuba, Canada and Singapore. And
now, clutching a vodka and lemonade, in a Liverpool pub.

"I have no regrets. Millions of people would still like to swap
places with me. Just to have been a cog in the wheel that led
to the greatest entertainment phenomenon of all time is
marvellous."

A big cog, nevertheless: had Allan not taken the Beatles to
Hamburg, there would have been no trained-up, hard-edged
group for Brian Esptein, and, more particularly, producer George

Martin, to fashion.

"If you've heard the Hamburg Tapes, they're pretty rough," says Allan. "If you'd told me at the time that this was to be the world's number one pop group, I wouldn't have believed it."

In those days it was John, Stuart (Sutcliffe), Paul, George and Pete (Best). No Ringo.

Allan Williams, ex-plumber and flogger of encyclopaedias, fridges and electric typewriters, was now selling a British pop group to the Germans: "If the lads hadn't learned their trade in Hamburg, there'd be no Beatles today."

Allan sacked the group after a revolt, led by John Lennon, which scrapped his 10% cut: "They were getting £100 a session between the five of them, and becoming swell-headed.

"I told them I'd taken them on when nobody else wanted to know. I wrote a letter saying I was finished with them. I also told them they'd never work again. Well, we know what happened to that… there's only me now worrying about a pension."

He last saw The Beatles together when they recording Let It Be.

Ten years earlier – in 1959 – he had first set eyes on John and Stuart when they chanced into his newly opened Jacaranda Club in Slater Street.

Allan, no longer a plumber, had spent £350 recreating a continental coffee bar but the women's toilets were covered in obscene graffiti:

"So, as art students, I paid John and Stuart to decorate the loos."

He also paid them £100 to build self-destructing floats for the first Liverpool Art Ball at St George's Hall: "All the Beatles came in fancy dress. I had photos of John Lennon in a grass skirt, which I've lost."

Their initial musical task under Williams' management was

backing a strip act hired by Allan and his then business partner Harold Phillips – the legendary 'Lord Woodbine' – who had come to Britain aboard the Windrush.

The first official Williams/Beatles contract perished when another of Allan's ventures, the Top Ten Club in Soho Street, burned down on its fifth day of operation.

History going up in smoke. But the memories linger on.

None more so than the night the Beatles topped the bill at the London Palladium Royal Command Performance: "That's when I really knew I'd blown it," reflects Allan.

"I threw a cushion at the television. I wish I'd had a brick in my hand."

He felt the same gut reaction when the group premiered their movie A Hard Day's Night at Liverpool Odeon: "I only went as the guest of the writer, Alun Owen, who was a pal. I passed the VIP room and every socialite who'd never wanted to know the Beatles was there.

"I was so embarrassed, I left early. It was pouring with rain and the Beatles were getting into a car to be whisked away to the town hall.

"I remember them smiling, waving through the half-steamed-up windows and shouting: 'There's Allan'. That really cut me up. They must have wondered what I was doing standing on my own in the drenching night."

The dream had become a nightmare?

"Actually, I don't think I could have handled it," admits Allan "I have a mind like a grasshopper. I don't think I would have gone the whole trip with them. But I'd done my bit. I'd created them."

Had Allan kept the Beatles under contract, he reckons he could have netted £25,000 back in 1961 for selling them to Epstein.

"That would have been a realistic price," said Allan, who had been brokering deals since he was a teenager. His father,

Dickie, was a joiner by day and promoter by night. His son and heir followed suit.

Allan's first promotion was a dance matching the lads from Bootle Tech with the girls from neighbouring Johnson's Dye Works. He could have been an entertainer: "There was a group called Steffani and his Silver Songsters.

"I passed an audition in my lunch hour, bought a one way ticket to Morecambe and had my bags packed.

"When I got to the bottom of our road, my father burst out crying and so did I. So I didn't go. I was only 14,"

Instead, Allan, born on Percy Street, Bootle, February 21, 1930: educated Beach Road and Central schools, Litherland; evacuated to Chirk, and returned home as 'uncontrollable', daily pushed a plumber's handcart down Hawthorne Road to repair war damage: " I was so small, people thought the cart was running away on its own."

He says the early trauma of finding out his mother was actually his stepmother 'has affected me throughout my life'.

"My real mother died when I was one year old, giving birth to twins, who also died. Her name was Annie Cheetham and she came from Waterloo. I only found that out comparatively recently."

Allan met his wife, Beryl, when he was in the Bentley Operatic Society and she was a visiting dancer from the Birkenhead Operatic for a production of Merrie England.

They married when Allan was 26, separated seven years ago, but remain friends. Their son Justin is 35, daughter Leah 24.

Beryl was on that first trip to Hamburg, when Woody nearly killed them all when the car got stuck in tracks in front of an oncoming tram.

The rest really is history. And it doesn't come bigger.

Allan Williams born Liverpool, February 21, 1930 and he is still giving the Beatles away.

FOREVER
A TRUE BLUE

Remembering Brian Labone
Soccer Legend

January, 1999

He was one of the great guys-on the pitch and around town. Yes, a football hero who remained visible.

BRIAN Labone and I have one very obvious thing in common: we're both twice the size we were when our paths first crossed 30 years ago.

"I've lost about three stones of late," he insists, making an immediate defensive tackle. However, he remains, on aggregate, a tad bulkier than when he captained Everton and led them out on the Wembley turf during the glorious Catterick years.

Nowadays, the Labone waistline is in the lunchtime care of the Pig and Whistle – or any decent city centre pub that hasn't been wrecked by a juke box. Weekends are mainly teetotal "unless there's a bad result and I have a heavy Saturday night."

Sundays are often taken up playing golf at Ormskirk (handicap 14), occasionally giving old pal Ian Callaghan a run for his money. "I also do a lot of reading," says Brian, nowadays divorced from his wife, Patricia, and living in Lydiate.

"I'm mainly into history and biographies." Perhaps he should write his own and bring us up to date? "My daughter, Rachelle, is 28 and the love of my life. She works for BT at Skem," says a still very proud dad.

"As for work, I flog insurance. You can be posh and call me a financial adviser if you want.

"I've been staggering around doing that for the past 20 years and I suppose I'm a bit of a landmark."

He says the pub, like the golf course, remains a good place to do business. "You make a lot of contacts. I like going around town - and I still like talking football. I just think they're tinkering around with the rules too much now. I know they've got to get winners of competitions but it's very sad when a cup final or the World Cup can be decided on penalties.

"I can't understand why they get away with so much cheating – people pretending to be tripped and getting penalties."

Never short of an opinion, Brian – 'Labby' as die-hards still call him – says he "used to be a very biased Evertonian, but I've mellowed a bit."

Today he does PR work for Everton on a Saturday, arriving at Goodison around 10.30am and leaving at 6.30pm. He knows all the present players, and they know him – of course.

Nevertheless, Brian had just stumped up eight quid for a ball for the first team to sign for a business client: "You don't get anything for free from Everton," quips the skipper of old.

"A lot of chaps still come to me with programmes from when I was young and slim and dark haired and ask me to sign them. I suppose there's a little bit of ego to it when people still recognise you."

And in his case, they do. For big Brian Labone remains one of the great local heroes.

One of only three guys - along with Neville Southall and Dave Watson – to have made more than 500 first-team appearances in the royal blue shirt: 533 according to the records books, 532 according to the man himself.

In the Age of the Striker, it's worth recalling how Labone had little interest in straying upfield in search of goals: "Besides, we had Roy Vernon, Joe Royle, Alec Young," he says modestly. Brian only scored twice in a 14-year career. At centre back, his job was to stop the other side scoring. Which is exactly what he did, using his height to head off an attack.

"This change to the new ball. When will it stop?" he wonders. "Apparently, the new ball is very difficult to control."

But what about the old, heavier ball being dangerous? "I headed thousands of them. Whether I'm going loopy, I don't know. Some ex-players do develop trouble. There's quite a high incidence of them becoming forgetful."

Everything's different. Not just the ball, but the kit even the grass: "Only the goals at either end are the same now."

Born during the blitz, Brian says football was the only thing that kept Liverpool kids going. "That was all we had, kicking a ball in Walton Hall Park. There were wide open spaces. Days when your mother would give you a bottle of water and a jam butty in the morning and she didn't want to see you until six o'clock."

The Labone home was No 1 Saxonia Road, Walton – "I still meet an old neighbour, Bill Roberts."

Prime conversations were always Everton's fortunes:" My father took me to some early games but by the time I was 10, I used to go to the boys' pen for threepence or fourpence."

If that seems laughable today, what about the wages? "When I signed for Everton in August 1957, the ceiling pay for a footballer was £20," recalls Brian. "I got £7 a week – very good for a seventeen-year-old. When I was reserve for the first team on a couple of occasions I actually got the £20. There was a £2 win bonus and a £1 draw bonus, and that was that."

There was also eventual anger. The players were considering a strike. They all met at Belle Vue, with Jimmy Hill chairing the meeting. The test case, says Brian, came in 1960 with George Eastham's transfer from Newcastle to Arsenal. Things improved but not madly.

"If a man was earning four figures, he had a good job," says Brian. "Even by 1970, I was earning £100 a week, which, if the average earnings were £30 to £40, wasn't a dramatic difference. Not like today. I can't even imagine going into my bank every week and having £10,000 going in. When I left the game you didn't have a million pounds in savings, and there were no pensions. So you had to work for a living."

He says he has no hang-ups about losing out on the mega-bucks.

Only in the late 70s and 80s did it go crazy. I would think players who just missed it might feel differently but when you're playing football, you don't really think of the money. I think players are a bit mercenary now but I also think they do their best."

But even to Brian, it seems an age since an Achilles tendon injury put paid to his career in 1972. Normally, he could have expected three or more seasons and then perhaps drifted into soccer management but it was not to be.

Labone was just 32 – with a very uncertain future: too young to become a manager, no longer fit enough to be a trainer.

A partnership in an electrical company had the cushion of knowing I could go on into my father's central-heating business when I finished football but he died in 1969, aged 51."

Norwest, who'd taken over the firm, said they couldn't find a position for Brian: "I hit a brick wall," he admits. "I got a phone call from a pal who played for West Ham, who offered me to go out to South Africa, but I had to turn it down because of my injury."

And so, approaching the Big 60, he continues to work.

"I can't afford to retire. Besides, some of the stuff they have put on telly now would drive you to work."

Brian Leslie Labone (January 23 1940 died – April 24, 2006) Played football for Everton between 1958 and 1971.

AN APPRENTICE LIVERPOOL HELLRAISER

Clive Barker
Actor, Writer, Author

April, 1976

A painter whose works sell for thousands of dollars – and second only to Stephen King as an international writer of horror fiction.

IT'S almost an insult to expect Clive Barker to put his dreams into words. Having founded one of the western world's half dozen mime companies, he's transformed hopes for a professional theatre career into action – literally.

"I had three years of reading words as an undergraduate," says Barker who lives in Aigburth. "You know, Tolstoy one day and Shakespeare the next. I'm not sure it meant much to me at times. Of course, one could understand it in terms of written prose, but I wasn't convinced of its real relevance to me."

His need was for something new, and theatre offered the chance.

"I'd always been interested in acting, right from my schooldays when I scripted farces with a friend.

"Gradually, my ideas changed and became more orientated towards mime. I helped form a group called Theatre of the Imagination. We played at the Everyman when the professional company was in rehearsal or on leave. I suppose you could have called our format multi-media, in that we used spoken word, mime and dance."

Barker agrees you could also call it controversial. The mood was often bloody, sexually outspoken and flippant about the Establishment.

He also says that it was not done for the sake of scandal or upset. "We dealt with issues and stories we thought needed to be brought into the open. I always remember hearing that somebody had walked out one night. It distressed me greatly and made me think long and hard about what we were doing. However, you can't put the clock back. I could never return to doing cheery farces. Although we were very young as a group – the average age was only 20 – I felt we had something to say."

Apart from the artistic satisfaction involved, 23-year-old Barker asserts that his theatre is socially responsible, yet is concerned with liberating attitudes and breaking new ground.

Over the past three years he has been streamlining ideas even further and has now given birth to the Mute Pantomime Theatre. No words, and some slapstick as the name implies, but much more too.

"We want to expand the potential of the form, bringing in an audience that wants to think as well as be entertained. When most people think of mime they think of Marcel Marceau, who despite his skill, views mime as theatrical charades. We are out to write long, short solo and ensemble works for mime theatre."

Barker's long-term plans include productions on the lives of James Dean and Goya. One can't accuse him of a lack of variety, it seems.

But his first show, which goes on stage at Liverpool University is called – wait for it – A Clown's Sodom.

Perhaps not surprisingly it caused one or two raised eyebrows when the subject of financial aid was raised. However, the Merseyside Arts Association is satisfied with Barker's serious intentions on theatre and has given an £80 guarantee against loss.

Its two main sources of inspiration are the Genesis story and a Commedia dell 'Arte scenario, The Curious Malady of Harlequin.

Barker risks understatement when he calls it "a very modern piece." With Lott as a get-rich-quick gangster and the Angel of Death dressed as a clown, you get my point.

The company realises that while people will pack a cinema to see the adventures of a killer shark in Jaws, they may back away from the moral confrontation based on an Old Testament tale.

"It's ironic, but people live very cloistered lives," says Barker.

"Art is split down the middle. Attitudes have driven people into dark corners."

Should the Liverpool production be seen to work, he wants to turn professional and take his company to London. "I want people to say, 'That is their theatre. They do such-and-such'. We are totally committed to the purpose of precision, clarity and economy in our art form," he says by way of summary.

Who knows, this eventual claim may be that actions can speak as loud as words at the box office.

Clive Barker admits that he would like to have been an artist. Perhaps that's why he's so interested in the visual side of theatre.

"Whenever we can, we use mime and dance to convey ideas in as pure a form a possible," he says.

"We like to communicate in this way as well as with voices. The image can often be of more importance than what people are saying."

The seven-strong group have written most of their material themselves.

These programmes all comprise new material, one being a re-write of Clive's play, Hunters in the Snow, which was done at the Everyman last year.

The two dozen or so songs have been taken out and the central character changed from an artist to a soldier. The plot still concerns itself with a struggle between an individual and the establishment, although Clive says the original script is now virtually unrecognisable.

Other features are a science fiction play, experimental surrealist dance and some bright and breezy entertainment through song.

"We feel that our new title is more descriptive of what we are setting out to do," said Clive. "It says more when people see the name on posters or publicity."

The group now feel that they are ready to show their work to a wider audience and have contacted schools on Merseyside, regional theatres and universities in this country and America.

Clive Barker, born October 5, 1952 Liverpool, England. Author, film director and visual artist.

BEHOLD HIS LIVERPOOL HEART

Sir Paul McCartney
Classical Composer

May, 2008

Sir Paul McCartney returned to Liverpool for what he called his 'revenge gig.' He was referring to a concert of his classical music being staged at Liverpool cathedral, where he was rejected as a chorister more than 50 years earlier. Sir Paul gave me an exclusive interview about his two Capital of Culture concerts in his home city.

FOR one he would be in the audience, and for the second on stage.

The former Beatle promised the Anfield stadium concert would be his "tribute to Liverpool".

But first he joined a capacity audience in Liverpool Cathedral for the northern premiere of his choral work Ecce Cor Meum (Behold My Heart), dedicated to first wife Linda.

"There is no better place for me to hold this concert than in Liverpool where I'll also get to invite my family.

"I have a lot of connections with the cathedral, having gone there as a kid and applied to join the choir.

"I got turned down, so this is my revenge trip."

The performance featured the cathedral choristers – the singing group he hoped to join in 1953 at the age of 11 – the Royal Liverpool Philharmonic Orchestra and choir.

"It is a privilege to be able to work with a great orchestra or a great choir.

"One of the things I particularly like about the Liverpool choir is that they are very committed.

"You get people from all walks of life, so I love the humanity of it.

"You get a plumber standing next to a surgeon, so it's a great mix.

"And that's something I'm interested in and have always liked. As on a train you find yourself next to someone who could be anyone. And it's like that in a choir. I love this coming together of various types of people."

He said Ecce Cor Meum, premiered in 2001 and commissioned for the world-renowned Magdalene College Oxford choir, was special.

"It was a great compliment to be asked to write something for them. They are showing you that they trust you."

Recalling his schooldays at Liverpool Institute (now the Lipa arts college of which he is lead patron) Sir Paul confessed: "I was not very good at Latin. But I liked it.

"I always used to encourage my own kids to learn a bit of Latin because it's the root of the English language and all the romantic languages. Sometimes, when you are trying to work out what a word means, you can go back to the Latin root and I like that aspect."

It would be the third time Sir Paul had heard a live performance of Ecce Cor Meum which won the best album award at the Classical Brits last year. He said: "I heard it in London and New York.

"But one of the great things is that these mark a bit of a night off for me.

"Everything I've ever done with music has involved me

performing so it is one of the luxuries that I can be in the audience.

"I couldn't play it anyway. And I couldn't conduct it.

"It's out of my range" he said, adding that he would never revise an orchestral work: "I'd rather write something new. You write something and you are supposed to be happy with it so I wouldn't go back.

"I wouldn't tinker with it."

Macca also revealed he is now writing a film score.

Paul McCartney's first classical work. The Liverpool Oratorio was premiered in Liverpool cathedral in 1991 to mark the Liverpool Phil's 150th anniversary.

"The cathedral was always looming over our classroom," he recalled.

"It was mostly finished by then. But they were still fixing on bits and pieces."

Paul later acknowledged the standing ovation for the Liverpool Cathedral concert of his classical music with a quip:

"This is the moment I have to pinch myself," he told the 1,500-strong capacity audience.

"That's because I used to arrive here on the 86 bus from Speke."

"I auditioned for the choir. They turned me down... but I am not bitter."

Sir Paul, sitting with members of his family, attended last night's northern premiere. He sat near the front, in the fourth row.

At the end of the 55-minute work, acknowledging five minutes of applause, Sir Paul was clearly moved, both by the occasion and by the setting.

He applauded the audience and artists, but then looked up to acknowledge the splendour of the cathedral he had first known acknowledge the splendour of the cathedral he had first known as a pupil of the nearby Liverpool Institute, now the Liverpool Institute of Performing Arts of which he is lead patron.

Sir Paul then took the microphone and briefly addressed the audience and musicians: "I would like to thank everyone for their hard work, the brilliant orchestra and choirs."

And he added in what was clearly a very personal message:

"I would also like to thank my dad and mum for having me in Liverpool.

"I owe this city so much – particularly this year."

Sir Paul returns to Liverpool on June 1 to headline the Liverpool Sound concert at Anfield stadium.

But last night, he was relaxed and in the audience for his four-movement oratorio.

The Liverpool performance was in aid of the cathedral's centenary appeal.

A note by Sir Paul in the programme confirmed the spiritual intent of the music.

He wrote that after being involved in a road accident with The Beatles during a blizzard when their van skidded off the motorway, the experience shaped his life's philosophy – "the faith in a benevolent spirit that, I hope, lives in the words and music of Ecce Cor Meum."

SPELL BINDING – FROM LENNON TO HARRY POTTER

Ian Hart
Actor

June, 1995

A good all round actor without any of the luvvy trapping. He later made it to the cast of Harry Potter as Professor Quirrell, teacher of defence against the dark arts.

FILM star isn't the sort of label Ian Hart would have attached to himself when he landed a bit part in Willy Russell's 80s TV series One Summer.

And being a modest sort of person, he still wouldn't… instead, it's other folk who are now putting him in that category.

The lad who started acting with the Everyman Youth Theatre and became a Playhouse favourite in such shows as the musical Cavern of Dreams, set off for Ireland this week to make a film with Hollywood hot shots Liam Neeson and Julia Roberts.

And tomorrow sees the release of the British movie Clockwork Mice in which Ian gets top billing as a teacher in a special needs school: the sort of school that makes Grange Hill look like Eton and Jimmy McGovern's Hearts And Minds school drama seem no more than a warm-up act in classroom chaos.

Ever since Ian played John Lennon in the Beatles movie Backbeat (he had already portrayed Lennon on TV), offers of film work come thick and fast. Five features in fact – including Ken Loach's Land and Freedom about the Spanish Civil War, and a quirky comedy set in Wales in which he plays opposite Hugh Grant.

"After Backbeat things really took off for me," says Ian amid much hammering as carpets are fitted in his London flat. A base in the capital? Surely proof of his new-found status as rising star. But before any housewarming party, he'll be in Dublin for three months working with the Hollywood glitterati like Neeson, Roberts and Aidan Quinn.

Neeson plays the title role in the film Michael Collins – about the Irish politician who was assassinated in the 20s. Julia Roberts is the love interest.

"And I," announces Ian, "play Joe Riley."

What? Forsooth – is it a joke?

"Well Joe O'Reilly, spelt the Irish way, to be precise."

And who may he be?

"He was secretary to Michael Collins, which means I am in lots of scenes, hovering around in the background, fetching files, and bringing him cups of tea."

But there's no hovering in Clockwork Mice.

Ian is distinctly front of camera, leading a cast which includes John Alderton (as headmaster), James Bolam, Nigel Planer and Art Malik.

It's the moving story of emotionally disturbed kids in the least understood sector of education.

Ian spent time at one such school researching his role.

Despite the contemporary setting, Ian says the film has a distinctly '60s feel to it.

"I suppose the most obvious example is The Loneliness of the Long Distance Runner."

The writer, Rod Woodruff based much of Ian's part on his own experience as a teacher. But there were some things even Ian Hart couldn't match.

For Woodruff was also a stuntman, being required to pole-vault from a train.

"And there aren't many pole-vaulting teachers," admits Ian.

Ian Hart, actor, born Liverpool, October 8, 1964.

OVERNIGHT SENSATION

Gerry Marsden
Singer/Songwriter

August, 1999

He made the Mersey Ferry the world's most famous sea crossing. He gave LFC their anthem. Not bad eh?

GERRY Marsden is the seasoned entertainer who has almost done it all. The first British pop star with his band to get to number one with his first three records: the man whose name in annals of Merseybeat takes second place only to The Beatles.

Someone whose songs have graced stages from Adelaide to Zanzibar and most famous places in between. A singer synonymous to this day with the roar of the Kop and the chugging of the ferries. The only rock idol, one supposes, to have travelled far enough in time and space to reappear in a biopic musical about HIMSELF.

So what else do you give a chap with a happy personal life, a career spanning 45 years and homes that spread from Costa Del Sol, via the Costa Del Anglesey, to deepest Wirral?

The answer – apparently — is a one-man grilling. The sort that's genuinely spontaneous unlike the telly counterparts with their planted questions. The sort where members of the public can ask questions they want - within reason.

"If anyone wants to know how much I make a week then I'll tell them not to be nosey," says the guy who's stuck with the music business while many contemporaries have retired, disappeared, lost their minds to substances, or even, sadly died.

An audience with Gerry Marsden is a brave undertaking, particularly in the city which, two generations ago, yielded up a lad with a ukulele who was to become a key player in a musical phenomenon still without equal.

"We were second fiddle to The Beatles. But I don't mind that. Every other band in the world was second fiddle to The Beatles, so it's never bothered me," says Gerry today.

"And, let's face it, people know I knew them. So if they ask me what John Lennon was like, I'll tell them.

"But the question I've already been asked most is what was it like to be an overnight star – to which I always say we started 10 years before we made our first record, so it was a very long night."

Once signed to a record company (and firmly in the Epstein stable of stars) Gerry and the Pacemakers took off with a vengeance.

They had grown from what was originally the Gerry Marsden Trio – a line-up of three behind Gerry – until the pianist heard a sports commentator refer to a particular athlete as 'a pacemaker'.

Gerry was the cheerful, jaunty character out front, proud of his flashy Futurama guitar, which he wore slung high on his chest, not unlike fellow Liverpool singer, Tony Sheridan.

"It was really because I had to play lead and rhythm and I couldn't see my fingers if the guitar was down by my knees."

And the gravely voice? "That was the pan of Scouse we had as kids. Nobody knew what their mothers put in Scouse in those days."

The Pacemakers' nearest partners in style were not The Beatles, but another local band, Ian and the Zodiaks. But Gerry and his group had that extra something that remains the difference between home honours and international celebrity.

How Do You Do It? I Like It and You'll Never Walk Alone all zoomed to the number one spot. Contrary to popular belief, Ferry 'Cross the Mersey didn't.

I'm The One went to number two. And there were other hits like It's Goin' To Be Alright and Don't Let the Sun Catch You Crying.

"But then it was a progression down the charts," admits Gerry. "By 1967 we had stopped selling records. The record market for Gerry and the Pacemakers had died."

Gerry had stuck with Brian Epstein as manager – despite interest from the Lew Grade organisation.

After the break-up of the original Pacemakers, Gerry was offered work in the West End – a musical Charley Girl, with Derek Nimmo and Anna Neagle. "It was a bit frightening at first, but Derek and Dame Anna Neagle were so good to me. They came to me every rehearsal and helped to relax me."

There was another West End job – a musical called Pull Both Ends – but by 1972 Gerry wanted to be back on the road as a singer – "I was getting letters from people all over the world asking what I was doing."

So he did what seemed obvious – went out and re-invented himself, travelling to Australia to break in a new band, then on to Canada and the States before attempting an English renaissance.

It was the culmination of eight years graft and still might not have worked had a company called Flying Music not seen the potential of re-packaged 60s Merseybeat.

Gerry was paired with the likes of John McNally's Searchers: "From then on, we were doing the theatre circuit again.

He plays what the crowds want. Never misses You'll Never Walk Alone or Ferry Cross the Mersey from a set.

"Most of the stuff's off the old records. But," he adds, "I do throw in the Robbie Williams song Angels and I might do Imagine because of John Lennon."

For Gerry Marsden, the boys from Menzies Street, Toxteth, who went to Our Lady Mount Carmel School, sang in the church choir, played footie at Otterspool and joined the band of the seventh Toxteth scouts troop, it's still a bit of a wonderland.

"It's a very funny feeling walking down Mathew Street now," he admits. We never thought it would take off as it did. We were just people writing songs and enjoying ourselves. But the future is tourism – and it's looking good.

I was lucky. I had my dad, Fred, who used to play a George Formby ukulele for inspiration. He'd go to Phil Bennett's pub every Friday and Saturday for a sing song, and then come home with friends – and carry on singing.

"I used to think then I wanted to make people happy like that. I can remember singing Ragtime Cowboy Joe on top of the air-raid shelter in Menzies Street."

But there was one prime inspiration for Gerry – the skiffle king, Lonnie Donegan – "I would deliver Echos in the Dingle and used to watch him on Six Five Special on other people's tellies. We didn't have one ourselves." But with friends Jimmy Tobin, Mathew Sutton and Tommy Ryan, the teenage paperboy soon had his own skiffle group.

"The irony is that Lonnie is now a great pal and lives about a mile down the road from me in Mijas on the Costa Del Sol."

But what drives Gerry Marsden? "I play golf, fish, I jet-ski but I don't do anything that gives me such thrill as walking out on stage. Every night is like getting an injection of love from these people.

"We were always lucky with our following. We always got a good reaction, never died on stage. I can't think of a bad experience to tell you."

Gerry Marsden born Liverpool still singing around the world. He'll Never Sing alone...

A SHINING BEACON FOR GREY POWER

Jack Jones
Pensioners' Leader

October, 2000

OAP's champ who's still happy to take on the fight

FOR Scousers, there's only one Jack Jones. And it's not the silver-haired balladeer from L.A

'Our Jack' as the generations of dock workers still call him, retired as Britain's most famous trades union boss way back in 1978.

For the past 22 years, he's had another career – as the pensioners' champion.

And that's what brings him back to his home city, to address a senior citizens' rally and march at St Georges's Hall.

"I haven't been able to get up to Liverpool for some years," he says, in a steady, alert voice that sounds exactly as it did on our TV screens during the most active union years prior to the 'Winter of Discontent'.

The man who, in 1975, beat prime minister Harold Wilson in a Gallup Poll naming the most powerful figure in the country, is now 87, and still both fighting and fit.

Nothing, not even the death of his dear wife Evelyn three years ago, has diminished an iron will to better the lot of his fellow men. It's a determination forged in the then antiquated docklands of Liverpool, with the sub-standard canteens and vile washrooms, during the 30s depression years.

But today his cause is what's called Grey Power – a label he says he doesn't mind at all: "There's definitely the increasing influence of retired people," he notes with quiet contentment.

"More and more are getting together. Groups and conventions are increasing in strength."

What's more, Jack Jones is still capable of giving prime minister or government a fright.

"We want this Labour Party to have a more human face and be more aware of the needs of ordinary folk."

James Larkin Jones CH MBE (born Liverpool March 29, 1913), known as Jack Jones, is a former British trade union leader and former general secretary of the Transport and General Workers' Union.

They brought us sunshine – Eric
and Ernie – Morecambe and Wise

Pop's Pacemaker
– Gerry Marsden.

Clapperboard, action – actor and director Ian Hart.

Man and boy – woman and boy (inset)
sex change celebrity April Ashley.

Hot shot star –
Arthur Askey.

A woman who doesn't mince her words – MP turned radio star Edwina Currie.

Awesome twosome – comic kings,
Norman Wisdom and Ken Dodd.

Barbra Streisand – actress singer
and world famous Funny Girl.

CRASHING INTO THE LIMELIGHT

Jimmy Jewel
Actor, Comedian

December, 1976

Still sparkling after 50 years in entertainment.

ONE of the jewels in the showbiz crown. They don't make them like that anymore.

Jimmy Jewel is 60 today. In a career spanning more than half-a-century he's had many breaks. More than a dozen of them have been broken bones.

The latest, into "straight" acting, has won him critical acclaim in two major productions – Trevor Griffiths' play, Comedians, and the Neil Simon comedy, The Sunshine Boys. Now Jewel talks of a possible stint at the National Theatre next year.

"Before Frank Muir talked me into doing Comedy Playhouse for TV nine years ago, I'd never thought of myself as having any potential as an actor," he says, "but now I've come to realise that if you're a comedian you must have something of the actor in you."

Despite the fresh summits, Jewel has spent the vast majority of his years entertaining in clubs and on the variety stage including some of the world's top venues.

It's been a family tradition. He started out building scenery with his father (also Jimmy) who died in 1936. A remodelled version of one of their sets will feature in the Empire pantomime this Christmas.

But the first time Jimmy Jnr. went before the footlights with his father in a double act he ended up with a fractured shoulder. It was, alas, the beginning of an accident-prone career.

In 1953 his ribs fell victim to showbusiness panache.

"I fell on to a whole load of suitcases and the following week at the Birmingham Hippodrome was murder – literally. I had to do this sketch showing how a pen would write under water. Every time I submerged into the tank, the bandages shrank. Getting them off afterwards wasn't so funny."

Back in the 1940s his right hand went crack after the sails fell off a windmill on stage at the Opera House, Blackpool. Jimmy was in mid-air holding on to them at the time.

Then there was the time at Torquay when he managed to swing through a matchwood balcony and land on a passing chorus girl. The young lady was all right; Jimmy broke his ankle and ended up in plaster for three weeks.

And five years ago at the Theatre Royal, St.Helens, two toes in his right foot were broken during a comedy called The Fickle Fly in which he played a middle-aged widower.

"I've been crashing into things all my working life," he jokes.

But there was never any question of following another career. His father, mother, sister and brother-in-law were all in the business. So was his cousin, Ben Warriss, who teamed up with him to form one of the best-known comedy duos of all time.

Jewel and Warriss went their separate ways in 1967 and Jimmy did, in fact, break into television.

But it's from his years with Warriss that many of his funniest stories came.

"Ben and I started out on about £15 a week and one week we accepted a date at the Argyle in Birkenhead for £12. It meant bringing up a load of luggage from London. We had trunks, cases, radios and golf clubs – the lot.

"There was Ben, his wife and myself. The train fare at the time from Euston was 12s 6d, but if you got a special trip train which meant you could take only hand luggage, it was 5 shilling return. We decided to try it on.

"I got out at Crewe and bought a second ticket to help the plot, but we were discovered and charged 33 shillings excess baggage."

We just hadn't got all the cash, I went to phone my father to see if he could wing us some money. And then a funny thing happened. When the operator told me to press button B, 18s 6d dropped out in copper and silver. I had hit the jackpot in a telephone booth on Lime Street Station! That saved the day."

Jewel and Warriss faced many a real-life drama on stage too.

Like the night Jimmy's 'pop' car – a Model T Ford built in 1913 decided to drive itself off stage, knocking the scenery down and nearly colliding with three people. It came to a halt by hitting a wall.

"It was one of those trick cars with pedals to make the doors drop off. I've still got it in storage. Ben was scared stiff of the thing. He wouldn't go near it. That night the delay locking system went wrong and the car went its own way."

James Arthur Thomas J. Marsh, always known as Jimmy Jewel, (born December 4, 1909, Sheffield; died December 3, 1995, London). Versatile British television and film actor.

SCIENCE FRICTION

Ken Campbell

Director, Actor

November, 1976

One adjective about Ken Campbell won't go away... Zany.

I FAINTED at the first performance – or was it an extra-terrestrial experience? It was simply planned as the greatest show on earth, which isn't a bad start for a company calling themselves The Science Fiction Theatre of Liverpool.

At the head of the launch is Ken Campbell, king of Britain's fringe theatre, and now firmly ensconced at the Liverpool School of Language, Music, Dream and Pun in Matthew Street.

The company will be acting out a cycle of five plays, based on the Illuminatus books by Robert Shea and Robert Anton Wilson.

It's a rambling story that rips through the Kennedy assassinations and a plot to release a virus. You can also meet talking dolphins and acquaint yourselves with a regiment of Nazi stormtroopers and a rock group bent on world domination. But don't let me give too much away.

Campbell, complete with brace-held jeans, a mixed grill in front of him, and a terrier munching bones at his side, says Liverpool has been chosen for a number of reasons. "People communicate here, they've got open minds. To appreciate these plays you've got to be a lover of all things new. And, after all, this was the first city to contemplate the image of the Yellow Submarine.

"I regard myself as an innovator. I had to get out of my roadshow because people wanted me to earn my living by it. I'm good at thinking up ideas, perhaps not so good at dealing with the format."

Two years ago he went along to a science fiction convention in the Potteries. It appealed to his pioneering mood and his wish to champion what he regards as good causes.

"So many of the people who matter are not interested in completely new ideas, only seemingly new ones, based on a well-tried formula. They like cardboard characters, not nuts and bolts men."

"We want to get science fiction into the theatre. If the literary board of the National Theatre knew the works of writers like John Brummer and others, they would not stage some of the rubbish they do."

It's because Campbell believes that such a breakthrough is necessary that he's inviting Peter Hall, director of the National Theatre; Barry Hanson, head of Drama at Thames TV; film and theatre director Lindsay Anderson, and a host of others to a day-long performance of all five plays.

Campbell says that science fiction writers are "brave and courageous – the sort of people I'd want to spend an evening with, the greatest company I've come across."

Kenneth Victor Campbell (born Essex, December 10, 1941) is an English writer, actor, director and comedian, known for his work in experimental theatre.

MERLIN CASTS A WILDE SPELL

Merlin Holland
Grandson of Oscar Wilde

November, 1999

Meeting Merlin – a charming and civilised chap – was like shaking hands with history.

IT COULD once again become the family which dares speak its name. Merlin Holland has spent more than half a century being Oscar Wilde's grandson.

His grandmother, Constance changed the family name to Holland to protect the innocence of Merlin's father Vyvyan and elder brother Cyril after the once lionised Wilde was sentenced to hard labour and dispatched to Reading Jail for gross indecency with London rent boys.

Holland was a distant maternal family name taken from a Major Holland Watson. It guaranteed anonymity.

Only in October 1954 – when they put a heritage plaque on Wilde's Chelsea house – did young Merlin, then eight, wake up to the fact that granddad was a celebrity.

"I was taken out of school and brought up to London," he recalls. "There was a big lunch at The Savoy. I remember having to scribble my name on people's menus."

But then there was family shutdown once more: "There were deeper reasons," reflects Merlin.

"My parents thought I might somehow try and cash in on or emulate Wilde. And in those days, of course, the whole question of homosexuality was something that was very thorny."

Two generations down the line, Merlin talks of his ancestor as either 'Wilde' or 'Oscar' or sometimes 'Oscar Wilde'. But never, during the course of our lengthy meeting as 'my grandfather'.

The apparent distancing is due to the way he now works – editing, writing about and lecturing on Wilde.

So what of the surname, referred to by Oscar himself in the biographical De Profundis as "that made great in the history of my country (Ireland)".

Wilde's father Sir William was the leading Irish surgeon of his day who invented the operation to remove cataracts. His mother Speranza was a nationalist poet and campaigner.

"If I do ever revert, I would do it for the Wilde family, rather than just for Oscar. One tends to forget them, and that shouldn't happen," says Merlin. "But a change would take a lot of personal courage."

He then gives me the first full account ever of his feelings on becoming Merlin Wilde.

"I think in England, I would store up a load of personal snipers and whingers. Whereas on the continent, people regard Wilde foremost as an artist with his sexual preferences as his own affair – here almost every article starts off: 'Oscar Wilde, gay play-wright…' I just shrug my shoulders.

"I used to say that to keep Holland would serve as a permanent rebuke to Victorian morality. But this whole business of being Wilde's grandson is something I found difficult to accept."

"The first 45 years of my life was very much NOT as Wilde's grandson. I was putting it off. But it was obviously going to go on being unfinished business, and unless I found a niche somewhere, I was going to carry on feeling uncomfortable."

"The only way to come through was to be accepted by the academics and scholars as someone doing serious research."

"I needed to be able to talk and negotiate from a position of strength, so I can stand on the same side of the fence as them, and look at Wilde as they do, rather than grinning inanely like a monkey in a cage. That I refuse to do."

And so it is. Personal mementos of Oscar include a copy of his first published work, the poem Ravenna, and a first edition of Dorian Gray in Latvian.

After five years "selling paper to the Arabs, travelling the Middle East and Africa at someone else's expense", 10 years with an academic publishing house, and a further 10 years running a ceramics import business with his wife Sarah, Merlin Holland is hard at work editing Oscar Wilde's letters.

He has also discovered 12 more poems from the great man.

What started off as a six till nine Saturday morning job, answering letters from Wilde fans worldwide, has become full-time. So much so, that he has given up his wine column for The Oldie and Country Life magazines.

And there is an apostolic succession. Like Oscar, Merlin Holland went to Magdalen College, Oxford – and it gets better.

Merlin's own son Lucian is currently in his third year at Magdalen, holding the college classics scholarship, and occupying the same rooms Oscar Wilde had at 71 High Street.

"It wasn't a joke by the college or anything", says Merlin. "Especially as Wilde's biographer, Richard Ellmann got it wrong and said 76 High Street."

Another claim by an Oxford hotel that "it was here Oscar Wilde discovered women weren't his thing" is less beguiling: "Its rubbish, and it makes me furious," says Merlin who is also working on a book about his grandmother, Constance.

"I have looked in great detail at her last years, and there are some astounding surprises," he tells me.

"Constance knew that she didn't come up to Oscar's level intellectually, and she could not give him the stimulation he needed. But she could give him a great deal of affection and love, which she was still prepared to do when he came out of prison.

"But I'm afraid to say it was friends and family who kept them apart."

Merlin refers to Wilde's upcoming centenary year as "the bunfight". It is but part of a gradual Wilde renaissance that has seen his plays back in the West End and on Broadway.

"He undoubtedly started the cult of the individual," says Merlin.

"If he were here today he'd be a permanent chat show guest, rather than the host. But he will never allow himself to be kidnapped by minorities. He was sufficiently generous of spirit to say that if he could help, he would, and then move on. And I think that's the way he should be treated by the gay movement."

"If people can come to an understanding of the subject through the sympathy they have with Wilde, then I think he will have performed a vital function for us to go into the next century with."

Christopher Merlin Vyvyan Holland (born 1945, London) is a biographer and editor.

MERSEYSIDE STIGMATA

Ethel Chapman

The Merseyside Woman Who Carried
The Marks Of The Cross

April, 1981

Mystery of the 'miracle' wounds... True or False? The jury is still out. But this article produced dozens of letters to the Echo.

WHEN Ethel Chapman died in a Liverpool home on July 22 last year, part of a mystery which has perplexed mankind for 700 years died with her.

For Ethel, at 59 the hapless victim of multiple sclerosis and diabetes, was the first Anglican to have verifiable experience of the stigmata - the peculiar appearance on the body of marks of the suffering Christ.

Her hands bore the imprint of the nails of crucifixion; her left foot was also marked in this way and there were marks like rope burns around both wrists.

Every Easter she had the same vision of being lifted up onto the cross of Calvary.

The first time it happened was in 1974, while she was a patient in Birkenhead General Hospital, being treated for septicaemia caused by a bedsore.

Ethel had become disenchanted with religion. Although she

had attended church as a young girl, the sufferings encountered in later life, and which had put paid to her theatrical career, had dulled her sense of celestial fair play.

That Easter night, Ethel said her prayers: "O Lord, show me in some way if you're there…" and later she was to recall: "In the early hours of the morning I thought it was a dream. I felt myself being drawn on to the cross. I felt the pain of the nails… I myself was in the Lord's body."

"Every Easter it has happened. The first two years it was Easter Sunday, then it was Easter Monday and after it was always Good Friday."

"Exactly the same vision. I just take it now as something for granted. I know it's going to happen."

That first Easter Monday the hospital staff noticed the signs of stigmata. Luckily, they took it seriously and told the chaplain.

The fact that we have so much detail on Ethel's story is due to the efforts of Ted Harrison, a journalist for the BBC current affairs unit, who recorded two interviews with her and whose book, The Marks Of The Cross, examines the case of this Merseyside woman and sets it against the historical background of the stigmata syndrome.

And he notes that when imposters and exaggerated claims have been discounted, there is still a hard core of what one medical expert quoted in the book called "profound uncertainty" that surrounds the untapped laws of nature and the depths of the inner psyche.

History has thrown up 320 cases of stigmata, beginning with St Francis of Assisi in 1224. The majority – around 290 – have been members of religious orders and fewer than 50 have been men.

Only 62 have been canonised or beatified, as the church is keen to say that receipt of stigmata is no proof of a person's sanctity.

Hence the ongoing deliberations of the Vatican's Congregation for the Causes of Saints examining the life of this century's most famous stigmatist Pio de Pietralcino of San Giovanni Rotondo, better know simply as Padre Pio, who carried the signs of Christ suffering on the cross for 50 years until his death in 1968.

Ethel Chapman was born in 1921) She was 53 when she received her stigmata. Ethel Chapman died July 22, 1980.

WILLY RUSSELL'S DONE IT AGAIN

Willy Russell
Playright

January, 1983

The start of a journey that would end in triumph on Broadway. The show that will always run and run. A man of words – Willy Russell.

WILLY Russell had done it again: that is, take a commonplace issue, forge it in the white heat of growing social awareness and then present it to the world as a masterly piece of theatre.

Just as Liverpool was the shop window for Educating Rita, so it is for Blood Brothers, his even more riveting and certainly more spectacular new musical.

It's a morality play, so simple in its premise that one is surprised it appears so vital and fresh in a nutshell, twin brothers are separated at birth, one enjoying the good life, the other never far out of the gutter.

Innocently, they befriend each other, teaching us much we may have forgotten to celebrate about the openness of the young or bemoan about the acquired prejudice of their elders.

And this is how Russell gets through beyond the bounds of Liverpool, to an even wider audience. In Rita he mainly did it with the theme of self-enhancement, whereas here he exploits the secondary idea of Rita, class, that particularly British obsession that just won't go away.

Blood Brothers offers no solutions, but it shows up the sorry results that gets to the senses without beating our brains out.

For Barbara Dickson, launched in big time singing by Russell's Beatles show nine years ago, there's much deserved acclaim for her first singing acting role as the mother. She really gets to the show's emotional heart in a most beguiling way.

George Costigan and Andrew Wadsworth, as the twins, are central to creating the musical's other great strength – a well controlled nostalgia.

And despite the ultimate tragedy of the story and its rather creepy preoccupation with superstition, Russell has the marvellous ability to be very funny very suddenly, be it halfway through a sentence or a song.

Chief catalyst here is Andrew Schofield, who narrates and performs a zany series of cameo roles (ranging from bus conductor and milkman to judge and gynaecologist).

With all of this – and obviously not forgetting memorable music, well played – a London transfer should be assured.

For someone who's not a nuts and bolts musician in a crotchet and quaver sort of way, Willy Russell's not doing too badly.

Tonight all those years of guitar strumming and pounding the folk club beat pay off.

Back in '75, of course, he received the Best New Musical Award for his show, John, Paul, George, Ringo and Bert, which started life at the Everyman and then ran for a year and a day in the West End.

"I thought of getting up and asking them what they were on about," he recalls.

"After all, the music and lyrics were by Lennon and McCartney."

This time it's different. It's all Russell – with a little help from his friends.

Out front Barbara Dickson, this time playing the mother of twin boys separeated at birth, one growing up an urchin, the other a nice middle class Nigel.

And, fundamental to the whole shebang, is Pete Filleul, a 31-years-old keyboard player, who's arranged, edited and set Russell's music out on chord charts for the nine-strong theatre band.

So good news again for the play-by-ear Willy Russell.

Obviously, most people now think of him as a playwright.

Educating Rita, written for the Royal Shakespeare Company, has become one of the most successful of modern plays. It's been made into a film with Michael Caine and Julie Walters, while on stage it's still being seen in Denmark, France, Germany, Turkey, Belgium, Israel, Mexico and Australia.

Its theme, of an individual striving for self -imprpvement, is universal,and Russell hopes that there are some universal themes in Blood Brothers.

He'd like it to be seen as "an English musical presented through Merseyside... and Merseyside is the heart of England, for God's sake."

What he's tried to avoid is having a 'play with music'. And the old American musical idea of the plot grinding to a halt for the sake of a song.

Stephen Sondheim is the best example of a modern musical writer kicking against the old format, although Russell says he's followed no textbook for Blood Brothers.

The idea of the story came to him eight years ago, and the tunes had been forming up over the years (his first public appearance as a folk singer had been in the old Spinners' Club in West Derby Road, when he was a lad of 17).

Singing was only ever an escape, a hobby, although he

reached the semi-pro ranks.

He'd thought of doing Blood Brothers for his RSC commission instead of Educating Rita, and also discussed the idea with Chris Bond, now artistic director at the Playhouse, and director of this production.

"He told me he wanted to do the show," says Russell, "but when Paul Harman asked for a script for his Merseyside Young People's Theatre, I told Chris I'd do a play version of Blood Brothers with just a few songs."

As it is, only one unaccompanied song went before the MYPT. company's Merseyside schools' audiences. Russell had thought that they were getting in an extra actor-musician for the job, but the budget didn't stretch to it.

So this really is the premiere, and all hopes are on Russell's pulling power.

There can be no doubt that the venture marks the focus of a lot of hopes.

"For me as a writer it's been a way of moving forward," says Willy Russell. "It's definitely not a one-song show. There's an hour of music in two-and-a-half hours of playing time. Hopefully, it could be the start of something."

William Russell (born 23 August 1947 in Whiston, Merseyside) is a British playwright, screenwriter, author, lyricist, and composer.

THE NAME IS BOND – CHRIS BOND

Chris Bond
Artistic Director

June, 1980

**From small acorns, mighty oaks. Licensed to thrill...
Bond... Chris Bond.**

FOR Chris Bond, the pressures of life are off rather than on.
You may think that part-responsibility for Britain's most
expensive-ever musical, which opens in the West End on
Wednesday, could prove to be a pretty big headache, especially
when advance ticket sales have been rather slow.

But the former Liverpool Everyman theatre boss can find
compensations. Sweeney Todd has already taken eight Tony
Awards on Broadway, besides doing wonders for the Bond bank
balance.

**"I suppose you could say it means that I can do
whatever I please for a year or two," he says,
but quickly adds: "Of course, it won't last
forever."**

Bond, his wife Claire Luckham, the playwright, and their five
children, will not be forsaking Liverpool for a posh penthouse in

the capital. Nor have they moved out of their house in Sefton Park or changed their rather toilworn M registration Citroen. "I've lived here longer that I've been anywhere else and the car is comfortable," says the man himself.

Bond's newly found five figure income really means more meals out and longer holidays.

"When the seven of us go to a restaurant, the bill can be quite hefty and this year we are having a month away instead of the usual week or two. We're off to France and Spain which will be nice."

No, come to think of it, our Chris is still quite frugal really, still rigged out to appear like a cross between a tennis star and a lumberjack, and still reportedly attached to an overcoat described as looking as if it was used to cover a motorbike at night.

The only real manifestation of a self-made schedule is a self - confessed lunchtime hangover, which rejects the offer of wine and calls out for soda water.

So with the pressure off, Bond can now indulge himself in writing a second novel (content undisclosed) and sketching out a TV serial about a Liverpool man who returns home for his mother's funeral only to involved in a murder frame up.

At 35, he can look back at an output of 30 plays and adaptations over the past 16 years, many done during his time as an actor and director at the Everyman: plays like When The Reds; Good Soldier Scouse and Under New Management, specifically belong to Liverpool.

But all those titles are now eclipsed by the words Sweeney Todd, a play which began life as a get-out.

"I was working as an actor at the Victoria Theatre in Stoke and there was some bloody awful thing I didn't want to be in," he recalls. "At the same time I knew that the artistic director, Peter Cheeseman, wanted to do a play based on the Sweeney Todd story. I volunteered."

Whether the Victorians, who were responsible for the early stage versions, regarded all this as mouth-watering or bloodcurdling is not quite clear. But what was clear in the Bond script – performed at the Everyman during the 1969-70 season – was its cracking pace and its blatant exploitation of melodrama.

We rejoin the story circa 1974 when the play was being done at the Theatre Royal, Stratford East. In the audience was the genius of modern musical, Stephen Sondheim. The man who guaranteed himself instant mortality by penning Send I The Clowns, sent in a request: Could he make Bond's play into a musical?

For our Chris it was manna from heaven: "I gave it to him and left it to him."

Suddenly, Bond found himself flying backwards and forwards across the Atlantic. At first New York treated him as something of a curiosity especially as he was swamped in that famous overcoat; then they decided they liked him and what's more they liked his work.

Christopher Bond (born 1945. British playwright, writer of 1973 version of Sweeney Todd. Currently lives in West Cornwall.

NORMAN CONQUEST

Norman Rossington
Actor

March, 1978

One of the most popular stars of stage and screen made an emotional home coming.

NORMAN Rossington walks briskly to the wall map of Liverpool. His index finger lands beside a green splodge which is Wavertree Playground.

"That's where I was brought up. Wellington Road. My father and mother ran the Railway Inn. I knew how to tap a barrel at ten, but I never drank until I was 30."

Now at 50, he's back to make his first professional stage appearance in the old home town, playing the lead in Trevor Griffiths' Comedians which opens at the Playhouse tonight.

The Playhouse publicity machine somewhat awkwardly describes our Norman as one of Liverpool's "most famous products."

It makes him sound like a set of Meccano or a 2lb bag of Tate and Lyle's sugar, but we know what they mean.

They mean that Norman's your actual born and bred Scouser.

When the Railway Inn fell victim to the May blitz, young Norman was evacuated to Betys-yn-Rhos, near Colwyn Bay.

But soon enough he was back, getting his first lessons in comedy from his mates in the 10th Wavertree Scouts. At 14 he went to work for 15 shillings a week as an apprentice joiner on the docks and then into the drawing office to get his National Certificate of Building.

At that time, theatre happened to take second place. "The Playhouse was the first theatre I went to. We came to see Swiss Family Robinson one Christmas. I've asked them to check-up on the date. It will be interesting to see if I've worked with any of the cast since."

"I can remember a young Richard Burton playing at the Royal Court in those days too. He was with John Geilgud in The Lady's Not For Burning.

"In my late teens I joined an amateur group called the New Theatre. I did three plays with them – enough to make me decide that acting was the life for me."

So at 20 Norman successfully auditions for the Bristol Old Vic School and the first thing they do is teach him "standard southern English."

"I was told that I had to get rid of my Liverpool accent." He has, although the Scouse is impeccable when required. "I hardly dared open my mouth for the first fortnight. It took them three months to convert my voice, but they succeeded. Now the land-lord at my local pub calls me a second-class Cockney."

With the voice "ironed out" Norman still had a potential problem with his height – all 5ft 5ins of it.

"Most people thought I was 6ft, because I've got a large head. But my height actually helped me. There are plenty of 6ft actors about."

But it was playing Private Cup-Cake Cook in Granada

Television's The Army Game that made his name.

He became one of the cult figures of Hut 29, a symbol of military chaos which taught the post war generation how to laugh out loud.

"Two series were enough really. I left in 1959 because I didn't want to be typecast."

Although he'd already made his first film, Three Men in a Boat, it was his role as Albert Finney's cousin in Saturday Night and Sunday Morning that was to broaden his public image.

The discarded Liverpool accent was rolled out for the part of the Beatles' road manager in A Hard Day's Night, and also for The Big Flame, a TV film about a dock strike, which was shot on Merseyside.

But when Norman made Hollywood in the mid-60s to work with Rock Hudson and Elvis Presley he learned perhaps the biggest lesson of his career.

"I was homesick. I used to buy all the English newspapers I could lay my hands on. When I'd finished with them, Elvis would read them."

"I missed everything about England – the people, the countryside, the way of life. If I'd wanted I could still be in America, but I'm happier here."

And nowhere is Norman happier than in Liverpool, the place he describes as a world-wide club.

Norman Rossington born Liverpool December 24 1928 – ded May 21 1999.

DON'T QUOTE ME . . .

Nigel Rees
Writer

November, 1999

**My first and still vivid memories of Nigel Rees date
from the mid-60s. He was my dinner table prefect at
Merchant Taylors' School in Crosby – a dab hand at
dividing a tray of dry sponge pudding and dousing it
with a jug of lumpy custard.**

NIGEL hated sport, especially rugby, which is why he prayed for
rain on Wednesday and Saturday afternoons.

Sporting prowess was the usual route to becoming a
'monitor', which is what they called the elite senior pupils at
Merchants. They wore gowns and most looked fierce.

By contrast, Rees N. was shy and quietly spoken. A shadow
of his future self. He had won his laurels as an actor in school
plays: "I never said anything in class, but that's how I'd show
off," he recalls more than 30 years on.

He fiddled with tape recorders, books, and wrote well –
aspects not lost on the senior English master of the day, Ronald
Shepherd, who put a coded message on his final report: "Nigel
must realise that there is a world beyond Crosby…"

This was lost on the parents – his late father was a life-long clerk for the Midland Bank in Bootle – but not on the boy. For the lad born in the shadow of the local railway station, there was to be no stopping.

But who would have guessed that he would pioneer News At Ten, present BBC Radio's flagship current affairs programme, invent an equally famous quiz show, write a number one best seller, and generally spend life rubbing shoulders with a new generation of movers and shakers?

Devising and presenting Radio 4's Quote Unquote – now completing its 23rd year – has been the cornerstone of vastly varied career taking in everything from comedy sketches to world-changing news stories.

But, as an 18-year-old in the summer of '64, Rees being specifically groomed to read English at Oxford, little did he (or we) know that a mile down the road at Catholic boys' school, St Mary's there was another sixth-former harbouring secret dreams of media kingship: John Birt.

Three years later, Messrs Rees and Birt were selected as fellow Granada TV trainees, based in Manchester.

At the same time one of Nigel's Oxford acting pals, John Sergeant, now the BBC's senior political correspondent, had started his career with the Echo.

"I was also offered an Echo job, but really wanted to be a broadcaster rather than a journalist," reveals Nigel. "I preferred a warm studio to foot-in-the door reporting.

"John, incidentally, was head-hunted as an actor by Alan Bennett. We were in a company that also included Terry Jones and Michael Palin. It was quite clear, even then, that Michael was going to be a star."

Although Nigel Rees would eventually find vent for comedy,

doing voices for cult radio comedy shows like The Burkiss Way and Week Ending, there were more serious foundations to be laid.

In Manchester, he presented John Birt's first pilot project on the Rhodesian independence crisis.

He started appearing more on screen – with fellow trainee, a certain Michael Parkinson, reading the news and doing interviews.

When Granada boss Denis Forman told Nigel "we see you more as a metropolitan person", he was despatched to ITN.

News at Ten was just beginning – with Andrew Gardner, Reginald Bosanquet and Alastair Burnett: "In those days, all the film had to go back the studio and be developed," says Nigel. I covered things like the dock strike, and most notably, the devaluation of the pound.

"It happened on a Saturday night. There is still a clip of me standing outside Number 10 as the Chancellor, James Callaghan, came into shot and an egg was thrown at his car. I was on that job with Peter Sissons."

Despite the fact that Nigel subsequently made a record 100-plus appearances as chief guest on television's Countdown, his most comfortable niche has been in radio – and, almost exclusively, with the national institution that is Radio 4.

During the mid-70s, he was the London presenter of morning programme Today as it transformed from laid back magazine with Jack de Manio, to the agenda-setting vehicle it remains.

"Jack was very blimpish, the real old style BBC announcer. He was famous for not being able to tell the time correctly. His scripts were written for him, his questions given to him. He used to turn up literally a minute before we went on the air."

Then the job was split: Nigel was in London, Brian Redhead in Manchester.

A picture of Rees and Redhead "looking like a garden gnome" hangs in the study of Nigel's London home in Notting Hill.

There was no love lost: "The internal politics were appalling," says Nigel. "There were several times I felt like having a bust-up with Brian. He was basically an ego on a stick, and dealing with that sort of thing as early as 4.30 in the morning was a bit difficult to squeeze in at times."

Nigel purposely left Today when he married Sue Bates, a marketing executive. He has always freelanced – a reaction, he thinks, to his father's one-job, one-place existence.

And something always turned up. When he told a BBC producer that he'd like to do a quiz, it was on the air in three months. "These days commissioning procedures take about two years," notes Nigel.

"I looked at my bookshelf for inspiration, saw dictionaries of quotations, and that was that."

It was 1976. Quote Unquote was born. A show in the same time honoured league as Desert Island Discs. And linked to the name of its inventor Nigel Rees, in the same way as Desert Island Discs was associated with Roy Plomley.

A forum for the famous: Lords and commoners, politicians, entertainers, churchmen and academics.

"Some guests are nervous. We try to reassure them. There is no score. Early on, we paired people like Malcolm Muggeridge with Spike Milligan, Terry Wogan with a professor of genetics.

"I had no idea the programme would run and run in the way it has. Now it goes along like a mighty machine," says Nigel. "It really is an industry. There are two series a year, a website and an international newsletter."

"Even if I don't know all the answers, someone out there does. Last week I said Shakespeare died in 1623, and it should have been 1616. People are generally kind in setting you right."

Does anyone come out with a humdinger of an original quote these days?

"I don't think so," says Nigel. "There is virtually no such thing as an original remark. You can always go further down the same line somewhere else."

Nigel Rees (born 5 June 1944 Liverpool). British author and presenter, best known for devising and hosting the Radio 4 long running panel game Quote... Unquote (since 1976) and as the author of more than fifty books – reference, humour and fiction.

DOUBLE ACT

Pat Phoenix & Alan Browning
Actors

February, 1974

Tempestuous and moody woman, lucky actress.

"NOW tell me honestly and I mean honestly, don't I look more relaxed than when I was in the Street?" asks Patricia Phoenix, lighting a cigarette.

I have to agree that she does, and that pleases her.

"When I left Coronation Street, it gave me time to do all the things I wanted to do around the house – bake bread, move furniture, look after the four dogs.

"And professionally, I felt that my life needed another challenge, win or lose. I'd like to win."

The challenge has come through two plays, Subway In The Sky and Patrick Hamilton's well-known thriller, Gaslight.

Pat played Subway at the Empire, Liverpool, as Dinah Hollander, a newly-divorced woman who falls head-over-heels in love with a US. Army major. In Gaslight, she's Bella Manningham, the victim of pre-women's lib domination.

"If anyone spoke to their wife today the way Jack Manningham speaks to his, she'd just walk out. But that's the way things were in those days," she smiles.

Jack is played by her real-life husband Alan Browning, who is making his debut as director.

In many ways, they're both glad to be free of the Elsie and Alan Howard labels that Coronation Street gave them.

"I suppose I can't help being thought of as Elsie Tanner or Elsie Howard after 14 years," says Pat, "but I WAS Patricia Phoenix for 20 years in rep before all that happened."

But now there are new horizons.

"We've been looking for a play to do together for some time," said Alan. "We must have read hundreds."

But isn't Gaslight a little over-exposed? Pat Phoenix thinks not.

"These days everyone seems to want to do light comedy, but I just don't believe people want froth all the time."

Patricia Phoenix born Manchester November 26, 1923, died September 18, 1986). Alan Brown born in Newcastle in 1926. In September 1979 he died in Stockport of liver failure at the age of 53.

IN THE MIDST OF DEATH WE ARE IN LIFE

Roy Barter
Coroner

June, 1999

**"It can be a very emotional occasion for everyone –
especially when two women turn up at the same time
to claim the body. A wife and a mistress."**

ROY Barter, Liverpool's retiring coroner, gives a quietly
Shakespearian resonance to recollections spanning three
decades. He has ruled over 90,000 deaths since returning to his
native Merseyside in 1968. Each is different. Each a human
story.

On the morning I visit his court, the last tragic chapter is being
told in the life of an old lady hit by a bus on the way to have tea
with her daughter. Verdict: accidental death.

The white-oaked Castle Street courtroom, uncannily like a
post-war Wesleyan chapel, is a place of teas as well as
resolution, where grown men weep, and coroner Barter
presides with the gentle humanity that has become the
hallmark of his immaculate and precise presence: a remote life
compared to the swashbuckling antics of the high court, with
whose judges he shares rank, and lunchtime camaraderie.

When not sitting with a jury, a coroner sits alone: in Roy Barter's case, a certain gravitas combined with the obvious compassion of a man for whom death has never become ordinary.

"You might get used to it in general terms, but I don't think I ever did when it involved little children." There are enticing menaces: "This time of the year is bad. The ice cream van playing its jingle…"

He breaks off as if imagining the possibilities, and having seen and heard it all.

He has at times, halted an inquest to refer the case on to the Crown Prosecution Service. Many demises are far from straightforward, but Roy Barter is known for being most wary of returning a suicide verdict.

This is because of both the stigma and circumstances: "Any coroner should be reluctant to do that, because you've got to establish beyond any reasonable doubt that the deceased intended to take their own life and succeeded in doing so.

"Two or three times a year, there are cases of someone found at the bottom of a block of high-rise flats where they had no obvious business to go. And very rarely does anyone see anything happen."

"You may find a raincoat up on the 15th balcony, and many people may say it's obvious what's happened. But my answer is that you are still not justified in saying it's suicide."

"It's possible that the person may have sat astride the ballastrade with that in mind, and then changed their mind and tried to get back to safety. But because the wind was blowing, they lost their balance and fell. All sorts of things can happen."

Stanley Roy Barter, born August 3rd 1922, went to Liverpool institute: "Jack Edwards the headmaster. What a very fine school it was."

His face breaks into a smile halted when he considers his ultimate fate: "When I came back from Africa, I became a governor."

He had spent 11 years in Uganda, eventually as chief magistrate, with powers extending to life imprisonment and/or 24 lashes: "I did once give someone 15 years and 12 lashes. It was a particularly nasty robbery during the cotton season."

In Rhodesia, they were contemplating UDI, but in Uganda, which Churchill had called "the pearl of Africa", the wind-down of Empire was less eventful. Until, that is, the emergence of despotic dictator Idi Amin.

Roy Barter, speaking always as he finds, remembers "Idi" as a senior NCO in the Fourth Battalion, King's African Rifles, living at the regimental depot in a town called Ginger at the source of the Nile.

"He seemed a very nice man. I knew him before independence in 1962. There was nothing to indicate future events... a giant of a man who adored the Queen and Scotland. He dressed part of the band in Khaki kilts. He had a great respect for places like Sandhurst. He was also a great British film fan."

Future headlines were somewhat different. Roy Barter says he was "most shocked and saddened" reading the way he would keep parts of human bodies in fridges. I just couldn't believe it. My own service out there was dissected by independence. The changes were gradual. Things tended not to be done as they had been."

"Eventually, I would leave the house and not see another white face until I got home at night. My European colleagues had long since gone."

"I had a premonition that things were going to go bad. I couldn't put my finger on it or say why or when."

Roy and his wife Barbara returned to Britain in June '68 to live in a house they owned in Ashburton, Devon.

Shortly afterwards, Amin toppled Milton Obote and swept to power.

Roy Barter had six months paid leave after a long tour of duty, but no job. His wife found the Liverpool Coroner's job advertised in the Law Journal.

A 12-strong committee, impressed by a set of references from Uganda, where candidate Barter had been responsible for 66 courts in an area the size of North West England, got their man. Salary £3,500 - good at the time.

He returned to the city where he had been appointed a barrister on the Northern Circuit in 1953: "Number 14 Cook Street. Almost next door to where we are now. I got six undefended divorce cases the day I was appointed. And some of them were hilarious."

Hilarious, too, was Barter's knowledge of Cantonese, learned for Army Intelligence for the Malayan campaign, but never used - except to tell a Chinese people walking along Great George's Street the time: "I've never seen a double take like it. They must have thought I was a secret agent."

In latter days, the constancy of Roy Barter's life has been his adopted Greek Orthodox faith, of which he became a serving priest (adopting the saint's name Alban): "If your name was Wayne, that wouldn't go down terribly well," he muses.

What appeals to him is the steadfast nature: "The idea that our founding fathers, under the guidance of the Holy Spirit, remain true for all time. It can't be true then and false now."

And so the values are mirrored in the life of this most popular lawman: charity and truth.

Roy Barter, Coroner born Liverpool 1922

SIZE DOESN'T MATTER

Unity Theatre
Merseyside Venue

April, 1977

The Unity remains Liverpool's most innovative theatre.

NOT every amateur dramatics troupe can claim to have had their stage and auditorium built by an MP, or boast direct links with an internationally acclaimed writer.

As it is, both Eric Heffer, later MP for Walton, and Bertold Brecht, the playwright-, were quite familiar with the workings of the infant Merseyside Unity Theatre, which grew out of the political heat of the Spanish war back in the 1930s.

Heffer, then working as a carpenter, built the first theatre club premises in Mount Pleasant, Liverpool. The Unity latched on to the new writing of Brecht, established co-operative artistic links with his renowned Berlina Ensemble, and presented several local premieres of now-famous plays like The Good Woman Of Setzuan, The Exception And The Rule and Mother Courage.

"Mind you, we should be ashamed that when we first read the script of his Spanish work, Senora Cararar's Riffles, we didn't think it was good enough," says veteran producer and one of the founders, Jerry Dawson.

In 1937, Unity, then styled as the Merseyside Left Theatre,

was one of 200 such groups fired by the issues of Franco's insurrection, and set to raise funds for medical aid and milk for the government forces.

Edgar Criddle, another of the founders, was organising programmes of sketches and songs to bring in cash.

He also had the benefit of two seasons as a professional actor with the Playhouse - "Those were the days when director William Armstrong would do something like Chekov's Uncle Vanya for one matinee performance."

W.H. Auden had said that Spain would be a testing time, but the Unity grew to be equally concerned with social problems at home and the threat of Hitler. Their goal was, and to a great extent still is, to awaken the working class.

"We wrote and improvised material," says Dawson, who has now retired as a drama lecturer from Edge Hill College, Ormskirk. "Theatre had become a middle class affair. It was all Noel Coward and thrillers. The working classes were only portrayed for comic relief."

Performing from carts, at park rallies and in trade union rooms, the Unity helped to pioneer (or revive) different acting experiences: the mass declaration, the 'living newspaper' technique of documentary theatre, and the liberal use of folk songs all played their part.

Forty years on, they continue to champion the new, the difficult or the neglected.

In addition to Brecht, they brought 'firsts' to Merseyside by Weiss, Arden, McGrath and a host of other names.

Above all, they feel that amateurs can afford greater risks than the box office balancing professionals, and can stage plays with large casts. "We are free of the necessities to put on commercial pot-boilers," Dawson insists with a sense of relief.

The group would like to see the pro-am divide narrowed. They have already achieved much with their own Everyman Theatre connections.

Edgar Criddle sums up their hopes when he expresses the wish that Unity "should retain an integrity and try to do things as well as possible."

Unity Theatrre. Born 1937. The show goes on...

LOOK BACK IN ANGER

Terence Davies
Film Director

December, 1988

Maybe not a name on everyone's lips but vintage to those in the know, and still making waves at Cannes in 2008.

SOMETHING sensational happens in Liverpool tonight. Terence Davies est arrivé.

Not that members of his family will be cracking open bottles of Beaujolais Nouveau quite yet, as they see themselves plastered all over the big screen at the Odeon Cinema in London Road.

Davies, now 43, has spent four years putting together two autobiographical sequences under the idyllic sounding title of Distant Voices, Still lives.

The trouble is the voices are distanced but to a generation; the lives are about as still as those of ferrets into Acid House.

Most of his family remain on Merseyside. When they see the film, some cry, some are displeased, although all gave permission to proceed.

The film depicts Davies' father as a psychotic brute. We see him beating one of his daughters as she scrubs the cellar floor.

All she has done is ask to go to a dance.

If the story were no more than a brave new Cinderella, it would scarcely matter. But Davies uses it as a mere incident in the catalogue of a physically abused childhood.

"He died when I was seven. There are still some things I can't believe really happened. Like being kicked all the way up the stairs just because I didn't do something he wanted at exactly the time he wanted it."

The real life legacy is Davies' hatred of unpleasantness. "I only have to go into a room to sense there has been a row," a feeling of guilt if he's late, and an almost obsessive pre-occupation with the truth: "I just cannot tell a lie."

But the suffering and the scars have brought their reward artistically. His film has been feted all over the world, from Cannes to Canada, and tonight it comes home.

And what a truly remarkable work it is: Terence Davies, rescued from the barbs of establishment movie makers by the foresight and generosity of the British Film Institute, has inadvertently perhaps, become the chronicler of an age.

What he shows is the Liverpool of the 40s and 50s, endowed with the sort of bleached tint used for Orwell's 1984, and presented as a celebration of photographic detail and love of imagery.

Not that it's sentimental:

"That's the sort of cosy stuff you want to remember."

Here the scenario is one of wars, warts and all.

Life is an abysmal round of births, marriages and deaths, held together by the Roman Catholic Church, the pub and the parlour.

Davies is still angry with institutionalised religion. "To think I once REALLY believed." He lost his faith somewhere between 17 and 22 and has replaced it with devotion to film, poetry and music.

"You can achieve a lot through anger, but never through bitterness. Bitterness corrodes you from within."

Yet there is so much left to savour: the cosy voice of the BBC Home Service Shipping Forecast, a million miles away from the glowing coals of a terraced house fireside, providing a sort of assurance that civilisation was intact; even the remembrance that 1959 was a hot summer, when people sat out on doorsteps in polka dot frocks.

But what about all the things we had forgotten? Stripy flannel pyjamas; billowing net curtains; hanging out on sills to clean sash-cord windows; chopping firewood with an axe; Two-Way Family Favourites; hospital wards lined with cold white tiles; Scarletina, once the scourge of healthy childhood.

And, of course, the war and the air-raid shelters. And songs about barefoot days.

Indeed, Terence Davies' film is almost the documentation of an era through song. There are more than 30 of them, sung with gusto or melancholy, mentioning things like the Harrison Shipping Line and all manner of local detail. But the result is not parochial.

"They really go for it in downtown Osaka," says Davies, now enjoying global recognition, and prepared to chastise films like Frank Clarke's Letter To Brezhnev and Alan Bleasdale's No Surrender as no more than "filmed plays".

He prefers movies which extol silences and promote picture content. "When you recall a film, you recall what you've seen, not what was said."

Certainly, in Distant Voices, Still Lives, Liverpool's post-war years are captured as never before.

I couldn't help thinking that somewhere just off screen, four little Beatles were growing up. And what happened after that the world already knows anyway.

Terence Davies (born Liverpool 10 November 1945) - film director, sometime novelist and actor

THE ACCENT ON RAW TALENT

Stephen Graham
Actor

August, 2000

Who's that with Stephen Graham? Well, if it isn't Brad Pitt Esq: shoulder to shoulder with Kirkby's very own Hollywood star.

BUT FOR Stephen, sharing the credits with a bare-knuckle boxing Brad in Madonna-man Guy Ritchie's new gangster movie,celebrity status doesn't look like being a nine day wonder.

The 25-year-old Scouser has been summoned to Rome by the daddy of all directors, Martin Scorsese.

He's been cast in a major role in Scorsese's next project, Gangs Of New York, appearing this time alongside Liam Neeson, Daniel Day-Lewis and Cameron Diaz: "I have to pinch myself so I know it's real… all these stars, and me, a little scally from Kirkby. I still cant believe it."

And while we're name-dropping, Stephen has just completed work on a Tom Hanks directed movie, Band Of Brothers.

As it happens, that's a serviceable metaphor for the mood on the set of Snatch, Richie's follow-up to Lock, Stock And Two Smoking Barrels.

"It was a great atmosphere." says Stephen. He plays Tommy, the Cockney wideboy sidekick to an unlicensed boxing promoter named Turkish (Jason Statham). "It reminded me of being a member of a football team – with Guy Ritchie as my Bill Shankly," says Stephen. "There was total trust."

Dynamic duo Stephen and Jason – appearing in tandem with EastEnders actor Mike Reid (who plays Frank Butcher in the soap) and others such as Usual Suspects star Benicio Del Toro – provide some light relief, and have been dubbed by Statham himself as the 'George and Mildred' of the underworld.

Together, they persuade a gipsy champion fighter Mickey O'Neill (Brad Pitt) to put up in a fixed match against the fighter of a Cockney king villain.

It all meant that Stephen had a lot to do with the American super star, on and off-screen: "I never thought I would end up in a film with Brad Pitt," he admits. "I was really nervous when I first met him. But he is down to earth and a really nice guy.

"We got on great, but I think he had a bit of a problem with my Liverpool accent. But that didn't matter. I just concentrated on turning him into a Liverpool supporter.

"If he ever wanted coaching for a Liverpool accent, then he could come to me."

Stephen is prominent on screen throughout the movie, and producer Matthew Vaughn says the role was probably the most difficult to cast, requiring a rare chemistry that mixed almost slapstick comedy with the right degree of terror.

"Tommy's a boss little character isn't he?" says our star, clearly pleased with the outcome. "A Cockney little brother type. At one point he has to save his mate, and show that has the guts to do it."

"But the character Tommy is not actually used to this world. I actually cried in one scene, which shows how I felt."

"But he's a likeable fellow really. He looks at the glamour and he wants to be a gangster.

"There is a thing about holding figures like that in awe. They even develop a sort of strange myth around themselves. It's all to do with the big cars and the money.

"Certainly, being a Scouser, it was great to play a Londoner and do a Cockeny accent. I ended up basing Tommy on two of my mates – one from Liverpool and one from London – and balanced it that way."

As it happens, casting directors found Stephen just a week before filming started: "I had already had a bit part – with just one line – in Guy Ritchie's first film, The Hard Case, which was a short for Channel 4.

"In that instance, I went along for the interview with a mate who was going for the part. I didn't expect to be remembered at the audition for Snatch, but I was," says Stephen.

He had first been noticed, in fact, playing Jim Hawkins in a production of Treasure Island at Overdale Junior School. The talent-spotter was one of his great heroes, Andrew Schofield, who suggested that Stephen went to the Everyman Youth Theatre.

"I was only 10 at the time. Andrew was already famous for playing Alan Bleasdale's character Scully. He was massive at the time."

By 14, Stephen was making his film debut in Willy Russell's Dancin' Thru The Dark, a movie version of the pre-nuptial stage play, Stags And Hens.

Stephen recalls: "I was one of the kids playing football on some waste ground as the main guy is on his way to organise his night with his mates.

"It was a great start, like an apprenticeship. I couldn't just go off and to a normal job after that. In fact, I never thought about doing anything else and, luckily, I haven't had to."

Work that followed included British thriller Downtime (with Paul McGann, and partly filmed in Everton): "I actually played a Geordie in that," says Stephen, "I've always been kind of good at accents."

There was also a role in the Margi Clarke movie Blonde Fist, stints at London's Bush Theatre and the Bristol Old Vic, plus television extra work – like playing a character smuggling tobacco in Coronation Street.

The ECHO has also played its part in what was fast becoming a classic case of local lad made good:

"You wrote an article years ago to help me raise the £3,000 I needed to go to America and up to the Edinburgh Festival when I got a place in the National Youth Theatre," says Stephen. "I was really thankful for that."

But he adds: "None of it would have been possible without the support of my mum and dad. They've been my backbone of support. They've always been there.

"When I was growing up, not many people round our way took being an actor very seriously. It was seen as an elitist profession, an upper-class kind of thing."

But in Stephen's house they did believe in him. Michael and Mary Fazakerley were convinced their son had a future in the business.

And it was as Stephen Graham he returned to his old secondary school, Ruffwood Comp, to inspire a new generation: "It was great to watch the smiles on their faces.

"Even if I got through to one person in there – just to say don't give up in yourself and your dreams – then it was a worthwhile shot."

And he says of himself: "I always had an ambition and a dream. I think you need dreams, otherwise there is nothing to aim for.

"And then, when you attain your dream, it can be a bit too much to at first, but it would never change me"

And it hasn't. For the big London premiere, Stephen has brought along his mate Lee (also from Kirkby). Together, they are sampling the plush pre-premiere highlife of being put up in London's exclusive Dorchester Hotel – traditionally UK base to more movie stars than any other hotel in the capital.

But that doesn't mean you cant be upstaged.

For Stephen, and the entire cast of Snatch, that happened on set… thanks to a small white bull terrier with attitude: "He was definitely the star," laughs Stephen. "Absolutely uncontrollable, attacking everyone and anything.

"I have a particular scene, near the end of the film, where I have to chase the dog. It was wild, to say the least. He had an accident on my lovely coat."

Stephen first went to London to attend drama college. His wife is an actress from Leicester, Hannah Walters. "And she is just like Julie Walters," says Stephen.

Hannah will certainly be visiting Stephen during his five-month shoot with Scorsese.

"We're working in Rome because they've just built a 1900s version of old New York on a film set out there.

"This too is a very meaty role for me, although he's not a nice character this time."

"An Irish lad, who runs his own gang, but works for someone

else. He works on the streets, and that's how makes out. Like the Artful Dodger, but much harder."

It will be fun on location. Escaping from English winter: "But I'll miss some things," says Stephen. "My Auntie Vera makes a lovely pan of Scouse.

"And I'll probably end up in a tent on a campsite. I don't think I'll get my own trailer... not yet!"

Stephen Graham actor, born Liverpool August 3 1973.

A RAY OF LIGHT

Ray Charles
Musician

June, 2001

A complete charmer – he phoned ME at home!

THERE'S music in Ray Charles' voice, even when he's speaking.

That's hardly surprising. Melody has been his life for more than 50 years, ever since kick-starting his career with 600-dollars of savings as an orphan of 18.

Now, at 70, when most men of his age sit slipper-clad in carpeted lounges, the world's greatest soul singer is preparing to tread the bare boards of Liverpool's Summer Pops big top.

"Liverpool is more than just another gig", he enthuses. "I'm really going to love this one".

And there's more than enough reason: "Don't forget, I worked with The Beatles at the Star Club in Hamburg", he recalls. They were the intermission band in those days".

Ray Charles – personally immortalised by songs such as Hit The Road Jack and I Can't Stop Loving You – reminds me he has recorded four Beatles' numbers: Something, The Long And Winding Road, Eleanor Rigby and Yesterday.

And he speaks of his Fab Four encounter as if it were indeed yesterday: "When I would go out and listen to them, there was always something fresh, compared with what else was going on at the time.

"They really had something, and always impressed me.

"If like me, you love good lyrics, then this was the modern poetry. The stuff those guys came up with".

Charles' chauffeur also came up with inspiration: "He used to drive around singing Georgia On My Mind."

The old Hoagy Carmichael song stayed in Charles' mind, and became his second million-seller after the self-penned What'd I Say in 1959, later to be copied by Presley, Jerry Lee Lewis and Bobby Darin.

Despite the fact that Ray Charles' last solo UK hit was Take These Chains From My Heart in 1963, he has stayed in the public consciousness like few other artists.

"I have to tell you, my career has been like a ladder, one step at a time. I have been very fortunate in who I've met and worked with. People like Barbara Streisand. I just love her to death, man."

The singer born Ray Charles Robinson, who changed his name as a teenager to avoid confusion with the boxer/vocalist Sugar Ray Robinson, has covered all styles of music – blues, gospel, country and western – even classical, when he recorded songs from Gershwin's opera Porgy and Bess with Cleo Laine.

"I think that's the clue to my longevity," he muses. "I always remember Duke Ellington saying to me that there were only two types of music, good and bad. There's a great element of truth in that. If music can do something to touch me and make me have a response to it, then that's fine."

Wylie Pittman, a café owner in Greenville, Florida, where Charles same in the Baptist church choir, had let him have a go on the piano, aged just TWO!

By seven – just after he was blinded by glaucoma following the trauma of seeing his younger brother George, drown in a washtub in the family's backyard – the boy was studying classical clarinet and piano.

"When I was a kid I played Beethoven, Rachmaninov, Sibelius and Bach," he reveals.

"But I got away from that because you have to play what's on the paper, and you cannot deviate from it. I used to make my teacher very annoyed because I would always be adding things that weren't on the page, and she didn't like that."

Throughout his career, he has always written and improvised: "Fortunately, these days, I have my own studio, so if I want to work at two o'clock in the morning I can."

"There are no limitations, and that makes it real nice when you get some ideas and want to put them down."

Even touring, the familiar piano of old has mostly been replaced by a synthesizer: "That gives me all kinds of sounds. But regardless of what I'm doing, I always take my bass player, my drummer and my guitarist with me.

"Your rhythm is your foundation. Everything is going to happen around it."

What happens in Liverpool is important: "This is a big one for me. I'm so glad to be making it at last, having had to call off a planned visit to the Pops two years ago", he says.

"I feel good, and the great thing is that I make people happy with what I do, and they make me happy with their response.

"I mean it's all still so great. I'm telling you. I think that is the best thing about music.

"My job is to make people forget their troubles for an hour and a half, and just totally enjoy themselves.

"Away from music I love sport – football, basketball and baseball – but what I personally like best is to sit down with somebody who can give me a good challenge at a game of chess.

"So when I come to Liverpool, if you are in to that, perhaps we can get a game going."

Musician Ray Charles Robinson (born Georgia, USA, September 23, 1930 – died June 10, 2004), known by his stage name Ray Charles.

THE ROYAL LIVERPOOL PHILHARMONIC TRIUMPHS

Michael Tippett
Conductor

June ,1995

One of the final public appearances by the then leading classical composer in the UK.

SLOWLY, he walked up the six steps to the stage, crossed the platform and mounted the rostrum.

In response, the audience stood as one and, put simply, went bananas.

At 90, Sir Michael Tippett – Britain's senior composer – topped out the Royal Liverpool Philharmonic Orchestra and Choir's night of triumph.

They had just opened Europe's biggest festival of British music, performing Tippett's renowned oratorio, A Child Of Our Time, in Saarland, south Germany.

And in this case, who needs critics, when the composer can speak for himself?

"I don't think I have ever heard such a good live performance," Sir Michael told Phil chorus master Ian Tracey.

Minutes earlier, Sir Michael, the orchestra and the choir had enjoyed one of the wildest receptions in the Phil's near - 30 years of touring.

It was a little bit of history in the making and a 100% all Merseyside quality export.

"I think it is very good for Liverpool," said Sir Michael, who wrote his masterpiece during the last war.

"Liverpool had the courage to recognise the work very early on. I think I conducted what was only the second performance, with them, in the mid-1940s."

The doyen of British classical composers held a bouquet of red roses above his head and said to the audience – quoting words from Beethoven's Choral Symphony – "A kiss to the whole world."

Nevertheless, the choice of A Child Of Our Time was thought by some to be controversial.

It concerns the story of a young Jewish boy who shot and killed a German diplomat in Paris.

His actions led to one of the worst Nazi pogroms ever.

However, Sir Michael Tippett has always maintained that the piece speaks for the universally oppressed.

After the excitement of last night's concert has died down, he told me: "This is rather special.

"I am combining the visit with a little holiday and a trip to my publishers."

British music specialist Richard Hickox also directed a performance of Holst's Planets Suite.

That, too, brought the house down.

Composer Sir Michael Kemp Tippett, born London January 2 1905. Died January 8 1998.

A 'SCOUSER' COMES FROM HOLLYWOOD

Mike Myers

Film Star

July, 1999

Always game for a laugh and proud of his Scouse roots.

MIKE Myers – alias Austin Powers, international man of mystery and occasional sex fiend – has no difficulty establishing his Liverpool roots.

For a global goggling the movie which has knocked Star Wars for six (netting $170m dollars in four weeks) there are two subtle reminders: Elvis Costello singing I'll Never Fall In Love Again, and a throw-away line about the 80s, mentioning A Flock Of Seagulls.

The Austin Powers sequel, The Spy Who S*****d Me, opening in the UK tonight, has our hero reversing the 60s to 90s time warp of the prototype madness of two years ago.

Now we are fimly back in the glare of post-Beatles' Liverpudlian waggery, with Myers apeing the stage-managed goofiness of Fab Four movies which are inherited by transatlantic telly and churned out en masse by the likes of The Partridge Family and The Monkees.

But if this particular Canadian boy wants to be a Scouse comic at heart, he can go one better than that.

Merseyside is still at home to a goodly number of the Myers clan.

Mike's late father, Eric, worked his way up from the shop floor at Dunlop's, taking night classes and being promoted to management: "That was a gargantuan, heroic feat in Liverpool during the 50s." says his eternally proud son in the most serious tone possible.

"The equivalent of a private becoming a general."

Apart from the knockabout fun that has marked Mike Myers' career – Wayne's World seems so very long ago now – there is an intensely private (and almost delicate) side to the same character.

In 1991 – just two weeks before his big screen pairing with Dana Carvey as two teen heavy metal fans running an amateur TV show turned him into an international celeb - Mike had flown to England to honour his father's greatest wish: that his ashes should be spread on the waters of the Mersey.

His family took a small boat from the docks and one of his elder brothers, Paul (the other is Peter), sang In My Life.

Michael John "Mike" Myers (born Canada May 25, 1963) Actor, comedian, screenwriter and film producer.

GREAT DESIGNS: LIVERPOOL'S LEGACY

Quentin Hughes

Historian of Architectural Heritage

December, 1999

Liverpool started modern architecture – you do realise that? The first question comes from the man I had gone to interview.

QUENTIN Hughes, the scholar and historian who, 40 years ago, made Liverpool sit up and take stock of itself, is that sort of person: out-going, opinionated, deliciously controversial.

Now nearly 80, he has produced the definitive and beautifully illustrated tome, Liverpool: City of Architecture – a selection of more than 250 sites affirming that this city has more heritage buildings than anywhere outside London.

And thereby lies a tale: "London has never acknowledged Liverpool," says Dr Hughes. "It's been partly envious, and partly dimissive through writing us off as something they don't want to know about. Historically, there was more contact between Liverpool and New York and Chicago, than with London."

An extraordinary statement from a man who has an equally extraordinary battering ram of facts.

As for global trend-setting construction, that wasn't the Catholic Cathedral, but rather St George's Church on Everton

Brow: "The first modern building in the world," proclaims Quentin Hughes. "The first example of prefabricated, factory constructed large scale pieces, made in advance, brought to the site, and bolted together.

"The year was 1812 – almost 40 years before the Great Exhibition and the building of Crystal Palace. But the architect of Crystal Palace, Paxton, knew Liverpool."

Just as Napoleon III once lived in Southport. His commissioning for the redesigning of Paris, with its wide boulevards, was, muses Dr Hughes, based on Lord Street. "He must have thought, let's make a Southport here, but rather bigger… trees in the middle, shops down the side, with covered arcading. That's my hunch. It's fascinating theory."

The new and magic ingredient for all this activity was iron.

"Liverpool has the oldest example of part of a building being held up by iron columns – the gallery in St James's Church at the bottom of Upper Parliament Street. That was 1774. And this use of iron became the basis, through steel, of 20th century construction."

Even more remarkable was the work of 1930s city engineer Alexander Brodie, who designed the first prefabricated reinforced concrete buildings. "These had their doors and windows cast into them in the factory, and became the basic form of high rise building," he says. "The whole of the Soviet Union, China, America and France took it from us, but we threw this wonderful opportunity away and went back to bricks and mortar.

"In the '60s (with the return to high rise flats) we had to commission a French firm to do a copy of Alexander Brodie's original idea. That's typical of this country."

There was, he insists, nothing wrong with the high rise living boom. And he believes it will make a comeback. "The trouble was the flats were badly run, they put the wrong people into them, and they didn't have the caretaker system," he says. "In France, every block of flats has a fearsome man or woman on the ground floor."

Indeed, adds Quentin Hughes, Prince Charles's outburst against modern design "threw a wet blanket over things and destroyed initiative. As a result, most of the best work by British architects is now done abroad."

Not that Dr Hughes is uncritical of some developments. He calls Liverpool's new Queen Square, "absolutely ghastly – a huddle of buildings, rather badly designed, placed cheek by jowl, with no thought for the spaces between."

And he calls the new housing in front of the cathedral, "appalling by continental standards.

"That's what worries me about redevelopment," he says.

"If it's going to be worse than what we've got, we don't want it."

But there remains much to celebrate. Despite 800 years of history. Liverpool is basically a 19th century city from the point of architectural merit.

And until the big clean-up there was the soot: "I showed an Italian professor around who asked where we got all the black stone. He was impressed."

Quentin Hughes was born in Liverpool in 1920, sent to public school at Rydal in North Wales, before returning to study architecture at Liverpool University – the foremost school of architecture in Britain.

His work and the war have taken him away – there were notable stints in Leeds and in Malta, where he founded the School of Architecture.

A former member of the SAS, in the days before it was famous, Quentin Hughes holds the Military Cross and Bar for destroying a Nazi airfield.

But Liverpool remains an eternal fascination for him. One of the guest lecturers during his student days was Giles Gilbert Scott, architect of Liverpool's Anglican Cathedral. "He took us on site and showed us how he was designing it, drawing every moulding full size, so it could be cut to shape by the masons. An amazing experience."

Thirty years later, Quentin Hughes was to become full-time lecturer in the same department. His book, Seaport, was the first to show the need to conserve great British cities.

He later founded Liverpool's Victorian Society, and remains chairman of the Mersey Civic Society. He also remains the greatest living champion of the Liverpool skyline. He is the man who taught Scousers to look up and be proud of their heritage.

And what a heritage it is. A mixture of great vision and pioneering achievements.

"We are a one-off city and always have been," he says today. "Liverpool was a commercial rather than industrial city. A place of shipping insurance and banking. Each of these interests owned a building and wanted to promote it. There was tremendous rivalry."

"There were entrepreneurs. They were interested in architecture, and felt that the mantle of the merchant princes of Florence had fallen on their shoulders."

"They had the freedom without too much bureaucracy. You could experiment here and get away with things."

During the Regency period there had been a plan to ring Liverpool with Georgian houses in semi-circle on the ground from Everton to Aigburth. "Everton was the best place to live," notes Dr Hughes. "All that developed rather like Bloomsbury in London or Bath."

This backdrop had the natural magnificence of the river. Water maketh a city, which is why Quentin Hughes says places like Manchester and Birmingham lack charisma.

He divides his favourite Liverpool buildings into three categories:

The aesthetic. "Definitely St George's Hall. Not only the summit of British and European architecture, but undoubtedly the greatest neo-classical building in the world."

The idiosyncratic. "Tower Buildings, with its large windows and military symbolism, being on the site of the old fortified tower of the Stanley family. The first steel-framed building. And the Liver Building... by the same architect, the first multi-storey reinforced concrete building in the world. Two great towers, with clocks and Liver birds. Nobody could sit up there and type. A pure statement of style and image."

And finally, modern architecture through technology, where he cites the use of iron, already mentioned.

The Pier Head buildings, he says, are, "a wonderful showpiece, an extraordinary act of bravado. I always say don't over-publicise Liverpool, or you'll get too many people from the south coming here."

But Quentin Hughes has also been a working architect. He designed the first house to have plastic piping for ceiling heating. Also the Wedgewood Room of the Lady Lever Gallery at Port Sunlight, and Greenbank House for Liverpool University.

And amid the welter of a still busy life, he nearly forgot to tell me,

"I once designed a cathedral for somewhere in West Africa. Whether they ever built it, I don't know."

Quentin Hughes. Died May 8, 2004

PROFESSIONALS ALL THE WAY

Morecambe & Wise
Comedy Duo

A black cat strayed on to the stage – spooky!

BUT this duo didn't need a lucky omen in the city where they first appeared together.

A very real part of live theatre – something that television can never quite capture or replace – is that electrical charge that builds up before a star appears.

Well, the audience at Liverpool's Royal Court Theatre seemed capable of doubling the usual sense of anticipation and excitement for two good reasons – Morecambe and Wise.

The silver-lined partnership is now 35 years old and still gleaming as brightly as ever. They possess very real ability to get maximum mileage out of a situation, a crack or word without running it into the ground.

Of course, there were a couple of standards without which any Morecambe and Wise performance would surely be incomplete: the face slapping, a flash of the hairy legs and so on.

But there was so much more too. Eric doing his ventriloquial act and Ernie's serious singing bit assisted by Eric on bongos.

This duo is so professional that it is only perhaps in retrospect that one fully realises how precise and polished their timing is, how slick their progression from one situation to another.

November 3, 1974

FONTEYN, MAGNETIC, CENTRAL FIGURE

Margot Fonteyn
Ballet Dancer

The dancing queen of her day. Legendary partnership with Rudolph Nureyev.

THE fairy-tale world of ballet weaved one of its most enchanting spells as Margot Fonteyn paid her first visit to Liverpool in six years.

But hush... whisper who dare, for this could have been Merseyside's last chance of seeing the world's most famous ballerina.

Now in her mid-fifties, Dame Margot, partnered by David Wall, danced three pas de deux from Swan Lake, Sleeping Beauty and Romeo and Juliet.

Rejuvenated rather than mellowed by time. And like a real jewel, borne before our provincial gaze too rarely, she completely captivated the attention – a central orb, surrounded by star dancers who can (and do) fill theatres in their own right.

January 27, 1976

STANDING OVATION FOR A LIVING LEGEND

Artur Rubinstein
Pianist

He shook my hand after the concert and said: "You are shaking the hand that shook the hand of Brahms."

WHAT a performance! What a legend! And when the audience at Liverpool Philharmonic Hall gave octogenarian pianist Artur Rubinstein the rare privilege of a standing ovation they were applauding much more than a solo recitalist.

For, to hear the great man play is to capture a little piece of history in the hope of carrying it in the memory through the years ahead. Rubinstein has had an international career since before the First World War and in the process has established himself as the greatest living exponent of Chopin.

The Barcarolle Opus 60, two waltzes and the Scherzo in B flat Minor showed an interpretive skill that went to the very heart of the music.

He was always in command, dapper, upright, still exhibiting tremendous power in left hand runs.

So many pianists seem obsessed with the clinically written note at the expense of interpretation. Rubinstein is different. He plays the music with his mind as well as his fingertips.

May 19, 1975

THEY LOVED IT YEAH! YEAH, YEAH!

Beatlemania recaptured for London theatregoers
Tribute to the Fab Four

London loved it, yeah, yeah, yeah!

THE Everyman Beatles were given a rafter-ringing reception in the West End by a star-spangled audience: pop star Rod Stewart and Pete Townsend, Superstar writers Andrew Lloyd Webber and Tim Rice, film director Ken Russell, Peter Sellers and many more came to remember.

There wasn't a seat to spare in Shaftesbury Avenue's Lyric Theatre as the Liverpool company reincarnated history from what only seems like the day before yesterday.

August 16, 1974

THERE AIN'T NOTHING LIKE THIS DAME

CAREER OF DAME PEGGY

Dame Peggy Ashcroft
Actress

Dame Peggy Ashcroft's brilliantly committed portrayal of Winnie, in Samuel Beckett's Happy Days at the Liverpool Playhouse, is one of those rare theatrical gems that you can wait years to experience.

SHE achieves total and lasting communion with her audience in this virtual monologue of a cheerful, resilient women who slips towards death within the blinkered naiveté of insular memories and hopes.

While Goliath stamina and utmost concentration are needed to merely portray the part, it is here also that we see Beckett's skill as a creator of lasting drama - to labour the mundane realities of everyday life with a formal brilliance that is also persuasive.

While Happy Days is well worth celebrating as a piece of invention, it's Peggy Ashcroft's performance that will stick in my mind.

November 22, 1974

A MILLER'S TALE FROM DEAR JOHN

John Bardon
Actor

A life treading the boards. And then 'real' stardom in EastEnders. A fabulous actor and such a nice man.

THE Liverpool Playhouse went into the nostalgia business when they commissioned journalist Bill Shakespeare to write Here's a Funny Thing, a look at the life and work of the legendary Max Miller.

John Bardon, as the patter-peddling clown turned the adventure into something of a personal triumph. The second half is given over to an intricately-timed and fantastically-delivered Miller stage routine, but the first act, the story of the comedian's rise to fame was rather swallowed up by the less intimate atmosphere.

Perhaps, too, it underlined the fact more play between Mr Bardon and his side-kick pianist, Zena Cooper, would have been welcome.

November 11, 1980

A ROCK AGE NUREYEV LEAPS INTO ACTION

Freddie Mercury
Queen Frontman

Freddie – perhaps rock music's greatest showman.

FREDDIE Mercury is a poser in excelsis: Even when he is standing semi-naked at the piano, lower limbs encased in red leather trousers, one leg is set in front of another, like a rock age Nureyev about to leap into action.

Every band has its focal point and in the case of Queen, now eight years into their reign, that means the man Freddie, a truly original stage persona if ever there was one; a natural co-runner in the male sensuality stakes with Jagger and Bowie.

His clichéd mannerisms, his rehearsed spontaneity are what the audience wants.

But gone are the squeezed-on satin shorts of yesteryear. Now it's the macho image, short hair and all.

Yet the voice is still big.

Queen's act, a totally theatrical experience, is a mixture of the exotic and the outrageous. And when Mercury is brought on for the encore, high on the shoulder of some hired Superman, the remains of the dry ice whirling into the auditorium, the mood has an air of the elegant decadence one associates with the cabaret of Isherwood's Berlin.

December 21, 1979

HOME GROWN INTERNATIONAL STAR

Simon Rattle
Conductor

He now conducts the world's greatest orchestra – the Berlin Philharmonic – and is the most feted musician of the generation.

I FIRST came across Simon Rattle eight years ago. The Liverpool Youth Music Committee had just named the 12-year old youngster as Student of the Year.

Since then the gifted pianist and timpanist has turned into an accomplished conductor of internationally recognised potential.

And this week he's conducting his first programme with the Royal Liverpool Philharmonic Orchestra.

He shows a good, expressive baton technique, keeps a cool head, and drives a sure course.

Nowhere was this more adequately demonstrated than in Sibelius's popular Fifth Symphony.

Mr Rattle offered us all the excitement of the music, yet at the same time never allowed the last movement to become a race of dexterity.

May 8, 1975

Encore. Ladies and
gentleman star of stage
and screen Lauren Bacall

Is there anything he
can't do? Renaissance
man – Paul McCartney.

Crisp and dry to the very end
– Quentin Crisp, a unique
star in every sense.

A tanner for her thoughts –
Coronation Street's diva Pat Phoenix.

Starry eyed as always the Monocled astronomer – Patrick Moore

Positively a stage
legend – Bob Dylan.

Dame, set and matchless – Barry Humphries as alter ego and wise guise, Dame Edna.

From Tokyo to Liverpool
what a way to go for
Yoko Ono Lennon.

FOR THE OTHER HALF IN THE SKY

Yoko Ono
Artist, Musician

October, 1988

Yoko Ono first came to Liverpool in 1967, as an artist in her own right, to take part in a "happening" at the Bluecoat. She returned in 2008 for the re-opening of the centre for the exhibition of John Lennon's art at the ECHO offices. A nice lady who's got better with age.

"IT'S a film that's made for you, not for me. I hope you like it." Yoko Ono, Japanese actress turned twentieth century enigma, joins me in the suite of a London hotel after the first showing of the film Imagine: John Lennon.

"I can't see myself getting that involved again, It was beautiful, it was also heaven and hell. And the ending was terrible."

No, not the film, she is opening up after eight years of widowhood, and months of putting together the celluloid testament to Lennon.

"There were times when we managed to have our privacy. We always felt that we were using

the media to plug peace, because that was important to us , we felt that we were on top of it. "

"John was very English right up to the end.

"We would watch British films together, and he would say: "I went all over the world and I can't believe I came back to Liverpool."

"He thought New York was a big Liverpool, with its docks and piers."

The film, which Yoko regards as the "ultimate" life story of Lennon, has its genius in Liverpool. There are all the unusual places, with all the usual people: the Cavern days; Allan Williams recalling the wild excesses of Hamburg etc. There is the inevitable footage of four mop-headed lads oo-ing at screaming beehived girls, jumping around and getting up to silly antics. By the time The Beatles played for the last time together, on a London rooftop, they were all fur coats and plenty of cash in the bank , and Yoko was already very much on the scene.

Many of the fans blamed her for the break-up of the band.

Today, she says, "we were engaging in such an intense exchange , that when people were accusing us, it all seemed to be in the distance. When you are totally in love, you tend to forget about it."

That intensity, with its bed-ins, did cool to several months of separation – what Lennon later called a "lost weekend." The film does not skirt the issue, but it underlines the final re-bonding in a way that even the sceptical cannot doubt.

Yoko says that although she set up the filming, handing over much previous unseen material, she did not put it together.

That's why she cannot say whether the other three Beatles were invited to appear in it, or whether they refused. "I think the result is extremely moving." she says "I don't think there is anything lacking. The important things are there, and close family members are making statements."

That includes John's first wife, Cynthia, and the son of that marriage, Julian. "The most interesting thing about this film is that it doesn't have a point of view, whereas the Albert Goldman book presents everything from a point of view. "You can imagine what I think of that book…" Probably the same as she feels about much of the gossip:

"People say don't stay in New York, it's dangerous. But I didn't take any notice of trashy books, but I wasn't going to sue them , as it would focus more attention on them. At the time I was feeling defensive and emotional, and I didn't feel like doing a book myself. Then I decided to pool my energy and do something positive, especially as I had promised to do something about John and release something new every year up to 1990."

The next project may be some songs which she and John had envisaged for a Broadway musical.

They are on cassette tape, not good enough to be reproduced for an album, but good enough to be published.

The film, based on more than 100 hours of Lennon interviews (which means he provides his own commentary), may have taken time, but the result is well justified by that. "Since John's death I have been in a strange position. I don't think anyone has been in the same position in history, actually. I have had to look at John's photographs and look at John's tapes and videos.

"It is most painful, as you can imagine, but I think I had to learn to block my emotions. And do it again and again. Still this film was very hard to watch.

"There may be other films made about certain periods of his life, but I regard this as the ultimate biography of John. It is a documentary. You can make up your mind about what you think about John by watching it. It's almost like we are still together, and I am enjoying it in that sense. People say to me "Where's that feminist Yoko? What are you doing with yourself? But I think because of the tragedy, I have changed a lot as well."

Of Mark Chapman, the man who gunned her husband down outside their home, she says "I cannot be emotional with hatred towards him.

"It was beneath that. I never thought it would happen this way."

"One rainbow has been seeing Sean growing up. I think it is a silver lining – something that makes me laugh.

"I think there is some blessing in everything that happens to you, and the blessing is both Sean and I are stronger for what we went through."

What pleases her is that a new generation will see the work. "Right now, that is my main concern: that younger people should be exposed to the film, and share in it.

"Newsweek just recently ran a cover story of John, and people are listening to radio shows about him. So you see, they can't kill him"

But there have been other tragedies for Yoko like the loss of contact with her daughter Kyoko.

"In 1979, around Christmas time, there was a call out of the blue. She said she was coming for Christmas, and John and I planned a big dinner for her. But she never came."

Yoko Ono has never heard from her since... But the future is the future.

"This year, Sean is moving to Europe, which means that I will have more time to be on this side of the Atlantic"

Indeed, there will be no retirement for the widow of the founding member of the century's greatest entertainment phenomenon; a musician, artist, writer, philosopher and poet, who when he died stunned the world into taking stock of his genius.

Yoko Ono Lennon, artist musician, born February 18, 1933 Tokyo, Japan.

HEY... IT REALLY IS MR TAMBOURINE MAN

Bob Dylan
Singer Songwriter – Legend

July, 2002

It doesn't happen very often. I had to keep pinching myself: Yes, it was Bob Dylan!

"LIVERPOOL audiences are always very knowledgable," says Bob Dylan.

Not that the adoring ranks packed into the Summer Pops big top will be trying to catch out a guy with an incredible 700 songs under his belt.

At 60, Mr Tambourine Man is gracing just one English stage in a tour that sweeps through Italy, Switzerland and a wide swathe of Scandinavia.

His fourth visit to Liverpool – the first two were in '65 and '66 followed by his two-nighter at the Empire in '96 – looks like proving the most memorable.

The biggest audience, certainly, and the creeping feeling that being a rockin' sexagenarian is sexy and cool in its own right.

He makes a pre-emptive strike: "I think words like icon and legend are just other terms for the guys of the day before yesterday, who nobody wants to know these days," says the one-time boy from Minnesota who became the singing voice of an entire generation.

And he adds for good measure: "You can influence all kinds of people but sometimes it gets in the way."

At Kings Dock, there'll be nothing between Dylan and 5,000 awe-struck fans but the memories that span a 50 year career – 55 if you count his debut at 5 singing at a Mother's Day tea party.

Today's audiences, he insists, seem livelier than ever: "They react immediately to what I do, and they don't come with a lot of preconceived ideas about what they would like me to do or who they think I am.

"Indeed, we seem to be attracting a new audience. Not just those who know me as some kind of figurehead from another age. I don't really have to deal with that any more."

But they DO want Blowin' In The Wind, even if it was written in under two hours. Some things just endure. The Cuban missile inspired A Hard Rain's A-Gonna Fall is another.

By the time Dylan played his first British tour in '64 – and met The Beatles – he was the unmissable artist he remains.

Singing he says, "is my job, my trade and my craft."

And he adds: "The stage is the only place where I'm happy. It's the only place you can be what you want to be. When you're up there, and you look at the audience, and they look back, then you have the feeling of being in a burlesque.

"But there's a certain part of you that becomes addicted to a live audience."

"I do about 125 shows a year, which may sound a lot to people who don't work that much, but it isn't. Someone like B.B King is working 250 nights a year."

But what kind of set can Liverpool expect? "Let's face it, some of my songs don't hold up live. I've tried them all over the years, and now I just don't do them. I have so many songs, that finding them is the least of my problems.

"I even have songs that I've never sung live," notes the guy who changed his name (from Zimmerman) to Dylan in '58 in homage to the Welsh poet Dylan Thomas.

To Bob Dylan, it seems that what he now calls "the architecture of a song" has become ever more important.

"The difference between now and when I used to play 30 years ago is that the songs weren't arranged. That's why our performances are so effective these days, because measure for measure, we don't stray from the actual structure of the song.

"Once that architecture is in place, a song can be done in an endless variety of ways. That's what keeps my current live shows unadulterated, because they are not diluted or jumbled up."

He says the critics "with 1975 ears" are the problem: "My songs lead their own lives," he insists.

"That's why people don't recognise them all. I have recorded my albums at various points in my life, with various musicians, using various instruments.

"If I was to reproduce all that, there'd be a hundred people up on stage."

But here's a guy, nevertheless, who can alternate between playing lead guitar with the band and doing acoustic numbers.

He says the two styles are "pretty much equal" to him, adding: "I try not to deface a song with electricity or non-electricity. I'd rather get something out of a song verbally than depend on instruments."

He still writes: "But more songs never get written," he admits. "I get the thoughts during the day. Sometimes I'll write a verse down but never complete it. I've written a whole bunch of songs, but as you get older, you get smarter, and that can hinder you.

"Creativity is not like a freight train going down the tracks. If your mind is intellectually in the way, then it will stop you. At times you've got to programme your brain not to think too much."

Yet there's no doubt that Dylan is conscious, above all, of returning to the birthplace of The Beatles – he an influence on them, them on him.

It's a mutual respect: "Of course Liverpool is famous the world over for its music, and I'm looking forward to playing there again as a result," he says.

There are other connections, too. Dylan's early mentor, the poet Allen Ginsberg, declared 60s Liverpool to be the centre of the cultural universe.

Recently, the papers of the late Robert Shelton, Dylan's main biographer (who was a friend of mine), were left to Liverpool University's Institute of Popular Music.

But too much nostalgia isn't good for the soul. Nor, it seems, is too much self-reflection.

"I never listen to my old stuff. I don't want to be reminded of myself or be an influence on myself," says the philosopher-songwriter.

"I want to go on, always go on."
And you will, Bobby boy. You will.

Liverpool Concert Review

Liverpool, never shy of shaping its future from the past, was given a special return present last night.

A chance to watch history actually in the making.

Bob Dylan at the dock is the stuff that mid-21st Century nostalgia will be made of.

Those who had waited a lifetime to see the people's poet in the flesh, were hardly going to mind going the extra distance, as the 8pm start nudged its way to 8.47pm, and we had lift off.

Suddenly, from the cavernous blackness amid high-piled PA speakers emerged the diminutive figure who did more to change the face of popular music than the Beatles, Elvis or anyone else.

The global Mr Zimmerman, who had changed his name in homage to poet Dylan Thomas, and then set about being the voice of not one, but two, and now three generations.

All the cornerstones were in place: From Maggie's Farm through to the encore Times Are A-Changin' – reworked and arranged for a new era.

The 5,000 pairs of eyes and ears in the capacity-filled big top were on the centre stage figure in the cravat-like neck-tie, black jacket and side-striped track pants who swapped guitars like lesser celebrities change racing cars, and zoomed through the music of 40-plus years.

And – even the faithful had to keep pinching themselves – it WAS Bob Dylan, alive and well. Slim, nimble and still with a full head of college campus hair that instantly reflects the 60s profile.

The voice is thrilling and unique. The barking nasal whine, perfected by teen busking on the New York subway, has in no way diminished in power or allure.

No-one (except, ironically Eartha Kitt) can so expertly trim tricky lyrics into shape around a memorable melodic line.

Like A Rolling Stone and Knockin' On Heaven's Door – the more classics, the louder the cheers.

So who needs to chat to the audience?

Not Bob. But there was a genuine surprise. He had brought his recently acquired Oscar with him and waved it at the audience.

The Hollywood statuette spent most of the night sharing a table top with Dylan's mouth organs as multifarious as his guitars.

The harmonicas were no after thoughts. They underpinned half a dozen numbers, evoking the genesis of the singer's folk roots.

And what breath-control. The absolute professional from the soles of his slip-on trainers to the tip of his still tousled hair.

Bob Dylan (born Robert Allen Zimmerman, May 24, 1941 in Duluth, Minnesota) is an American singer-songwriter, author, poet.

STAR MAN

Patrick Moore
Astronomer, Author

February, 2000

Patrick Moore brings perspective to life – at his usual velocity of 220-words per minute.

"LOOK at it this way. Our sun is one of a hundred thousand million stars in our galaxy, and there are thousand of millions of galaxies."

The man with his monocled eye on the sky is not talking choccy bars. His stock-take is on planets, meteors, black holes and worlds with end.

And there is no end.

"We see objects so far away that we view them as they used to be before the Earth existed.

"Our sun is a very ordinary kind of star," continues the learned doctor.

"I have very good evidence that there are other worlds going around these other stars. So there must be billions upon billions of other worlds where life can exist."

In a nutshell – and in this case unprompted – Patrick Moore has answered the question he is most often asked. Is there other intelligence out there?

Yet it appears he is not even sure whether intelligent life exists on Earth.

Hence his declaration that "the Millennium is total rubbish. It means that every crackpot is coming out of the woodwork: astrologers, flying saucerists, as well as creation and conspiracy theorists."

He adds for good measure: "There's no astronomical interest in the Millennium. Besides, there is no such thing as the year nought. The government got it wrong, but you'd expect that."

There's a guffaw, as the scientist-turned-showman draws breath before insisting once more that in terms of time – real or imagined – the year 2000 means nothing.

Nor, one imagines, does the fact that the good doctor lives in a 13th century thatched house in deepest Sussex.

However, one thing he's sure of is being 77-years-old – in Earth years.

So not bad to be going around the UK in 80 days evangelising about numerous space heroes – everyone from Ptolemy the Greek to comet celebrity Edmond Halley.

"Halley was very much an all-rounder, you know," he says.

"He was the second Astronomer Royal, and expert on defences, and he invented a type of diving bell. If he hadn't lived at the same time as Newton, he would have been more famous."

But TV has brought unrivalled fame to the crumpled man with the raging eyebrows: Patrick Moore's Sky At Night is the longest running programme on the box.

He has, however, been contemplating existence since the age

of six, when he picked up one of his mother's books: "It was The Story of the Solar System, by GF Chambers, price sixpence. I still have it."

The only son of an army officer, Patrick also inherited a love of music from his mother, who had trained as an opera singer in Italy.

By nine, he could read and write music, entirely self-taught. His first compostion – there are now more than 70, including marches, suites, numerous waltzes and a comic opera called Galileo – was produced as an 11-year-old.

Two years later, he has also published his first article on astronomy.

After war service as a navigator in bomber command, he wrote a book called A Guide To The Moon.

Although he is a leading world authority on the planet Neptune, and has now published more than 100 books, the Moon remains his favourite subject. He did the television commentary for man's first landing.

Indeed, he is a Moon-mapper with the International Astronomical Union: "So I am an astronomer in my own right," the doctor tells anyone who ventures to suggest he is a 'tabloid' scientist.

When ice was reported on the Moon, our man remained sceptical.

"Even if it's true, I don't know how it got there," he told me. "And if so, it would probably only fill a lake the size of the Serpentine."

A nice image, which is what he excels at. After 42 years presenting The Sky At Night, Patrick Moore is nothing less than a British institution. The image of him playing the xylophone on the Morecambe and Wise show is imprinted on the minds of those of a certain age.

Patrick's many honours (OBE followed by CBE, four doctorates, past presidency of the British Astronomical Association, and director of the Armagh Planetarium) also include a Fellowship from the Liverpool John Moores University. He helped their astro-physics department raise money to set up a network of telescopes, including one to be built in the Canary Islands.

He describes the venture as "a great thing for the city," and stresses: "There is no question about Liverpool's contribution to space study. I think everyone can be very proud of it."

But there was a surprise: "I joined the university committee and found myself voted in as chairman. I did my job and I think it worked very well. But I also think my role there is finished now.

"If life can appear elsewhere, I think we'll find out very soon. We'll get our specimens back from Mars. No little green men, no plants. But if there is any kind of life there at all, it will prove that life will appear when it can."

Things are so much clearer now. Or are they?

"If you look at the sun you are seeing it as it was eight and a half minutes ago.

"I've always lived with these figures. I can't appreciate them. But neither can anyone else," he says, at last surrendering to human insignificance.

Sir Alfred Patrick Caldwell-Moore, astronomer CBE, HonFRS, FRAS (born 4 March 1923 in Pinner),

RENAISSANCE MAN

Paul McCartney
Musician, Poet and Painter

January, 2002

The broad brushstrokes of the Everyman as artist.

PAUL McCartney can paint, and Liverpool isn't just doing an old Beatle a favour by showing his pictures.

Nor, according to the man who is hanging McCartney art on the walls for all to see, is it a case of cashing in on celebrity to underpin the £4m refit of the Walker Gallery which re-opens in two weeks.

Michael Simpson, 40, the Walker's head of fine art, says: "I really think Paul's work is of real quality, and we would have taken it seriously no matter who it is by."

Seventy pictures – about 10% of McCartney's output since he started painting as a hobby during the mid-80s – will be seen in Liverpool this summer.

They are almost exclusively oils, with the bonus of two photographic works – Paul's latest activity as self-styled Renaissance Man.

Says Michael Simpson: "None of this will be seen in London, which we are very chuffed about. Anyone who wants to see it will have to come to Liverpool."

A book on McCartney's art, featuring some of the pictures, has just been published.

The only time the public has ever seen any Macca pictures was in the provisional German town of Siegen in 1999.

" It was a deliberate decision by Paul for a low-key venue away from the UK," notes Michael.

"You can't blame him. An artist working in a studio never quite knows what other people are going to say when they see the work. But Paul McCartney is a genuinely modest man when it comes to his art."

It was after the German preview that the late Sir Richard Foster, the then director of Merseyside's museums and galleries, decided to try and bring McCartney's art to Liverpool.

Michael Simpson, visited studios in Paul's homes, and a London warehouse where most of the pictures are stored.

"I was never a Beatles fan," says Michael, squashing any idea that he might have been over-awed by past musical glories.

"There are two types of celebrity painter: those who trade on the fact, and those who are actually so creative that things just bubble out of them in all sorts of ways."

"Paul is in the latter category. He is one of the most creative people I have ever met.

"It's quite humbling to be in the company of someone who's so constantly involved in different artistic things."

The pictures to be seen in Liverpool, include one showing the Speke streets of McCartney's childhood, and another of his late wife, Linda.

The best, says Michael, is a large work, Big Mountain Face, showing what looks like a human face formed in an Alpine cliff.

"This was painted recently, and shows the artist at his most confident."

Michael's time with Paul McCartney gave him an insight into the ex-Beatles methods: "Paul doesn't have a set pattern in doing his paintings, and he doesn't paint every day.

"He may be in his New York apartment or one of his homes in England and just decide to pick up a brush. It all depends what sort of mood he's in."

"Previously, he had never been working towards an official exhibition, so painting has become important.

"Before, it had been a hobby whn he wanted a break from music. I love working with contemporary artists, and what has made this such a lovely joy is that Paul is so genuine about it all.

"He's always going into galleries on his travels. He's probably seen more art than I have. He particularly likes the work of the Belgian surrealist Rene Magritte, and the late American abstract expressionist Willem de Kooning, whom he met more than 20 years ago.

"That said, he has been in the company of artists ever since his Beatles days. His knowledge is very impressive."

And it wasn't just John Lennon and Stuart Sutcliffe's Liverpool art college friendship which sparked the interest.

McCartney and Lennon would spend teenage after-hours wandering around the Walker Gallery.

"Paul was instrumental in getting Peter Blake to do the Sgt. Pepper record sleeve and Richard Hamilton to do the White Album," says Michael.

"Now Paul's art is going off in a whole new direction, and it's a brave decision to show some of these brand new works in Liverpool.

"He genuinely loves coming back to his home city, and he wants the exhibition here to be the best.

"For my part, I wanted to show diversity of what he has done: large, small, highly coloured, black and white, abstract and figurative.

"He really has experimented, and I am convinced that painting is now a key element in his creative life, and that he uses it to express how he feels."

Sir James Paul McCartney, MBE (born Liverpool June 18 1942) is an English rock singer, bass guitarist, songwriter, composer, multi-instrumentalist, entrepreneur, record producer, film producer and animal-rights activist.

CRISP TO THE VERY END

Quentin Crisp
Author, Critic, Actor

November 20, 1999

Seventy-two hours after this interview, Quentin Crisp died.

ON September 6, 1981, Quentin Crisp, then 72, did a one-man show at Liverpool's Royal Court Theatre – and promptly left for a new life in America: "What a way to go," he said in gratitude to his Merseyside fans at the time.

That, it was presumed, was the last we'd see of the blue rinsed Mr Crisp, graciously swaying from the ankles up, and pedalling his most famous lifestyle line: "Don't bother keeping up with the Joneses. Drag them down to your level, it's cheaper."

Wrong!

Now, Crisp, billed as Britain's most famous gay icon and most quoted ex-patriot, returns to the city for an evening at the Unity Theatre. An Audience With Quentin Crisp sold out in two hours. Unscripted, unrehearsed and unhurried, it will take the form of a chat.

For a man who lived in obscurity until he was 68, emigrated 18 years ago – seven years beyond pensionable age – and will be 91 on Christmas Day, Crisp seems unfazed at the prospect of a fortnight's British tour.

His forte is intrigue (or the thinking person's gossip): "I've just come from having lunch with a man who used to be an MP in your country", he teases, returning late to his New York abode.

Clearly, to the gender-challenging child born of middle-class, middle-brow parents in Sutton, Surrey, during the reign of King Edward VII, the United States is now home. He the resident alien, myself the intrusive interviewer.

But two decades on from when I first visited him in his flat in Beaufort Street, Chelsea, the lifestyle remains the same: one shabby room, underlining that old Crispian adage about doing away with domestic ritual as no more dust settles after four years.

A lodging in a rooming house on the same block as a gang of Hell's Angels along Manhattan's Lower East Side: "You can't get any lower. New Yorkers like to frighten you with New York, but I've never felt any danger", confides a now venerable Q.C.

The voice has become deeper and darker, like an un-oiled rachet. The skin has become translucent, as that around the gills of a fish. There is a quiet restraint with Barbara Cartland would be advised to emulate.

The lust for life is still there: "There has been a massive change in everything except me", he reflects.

"But you are always welcome in America, which is what's so wonderful. When I arrived, I just got myself an immigration lawyer. Here everyone is specialised – lawyers, doctors, you name it.

"She took me to an office on the right day, when there was a man who was sympathetic to my case. I was only there a quarter-of-an-hour when they gave me a Green Card, which is actually bright blue."

Then what?

"Nothing. I have never applied to be a naturalised citizen

because I can't learn all the stuff – a terrible amount of American political history. They want you to know what you are swearing allegiance to, which is natural enough. But they don't seem to mind how long you stay with a Green Card, as long as you don't make trouble."

He went to America disillusioned: "I know that the English don't like me, I wouldn't say I was popular. I suppose I am coming back somewhat reluctantly. I work for an ex-policeman who runs a company called Authors on Tour."

America was an escape from the name-calling that had plagued him since the 1920s, when his youthful effeminate manner marked him out for ridicule. The then flame-red hair, the lipstick, the entire demeanour. Violence was a daily threat.

For 35 years he worked as an artist's model – hence the biog title, The Naked Civil Servant. When the book was made into a television film, starring John Hurt, Crisp emerged into the limelight with one minor reservation: a quietly spoken "sod off" in the script – because in real life he never swears.

"My weapon is my politeness. Without it I would have been killed." Indeed, he adds, in Russia, he would have been shot.

Since a teenager, he "has lived by kind permission of the universe." Until the book, he had never earned more than £12 a week in his life, describing himself to income tax inspectors as a "retired waif".

With fame he learned to wear an expression of fatuous affability joining what he called "the nodding and smiling racket."

No more poor man's coffee made on an old gas stove, and biscuits out of a rusting tin. Top restrateurs liked the idea of QC adorning their tables.

At the height of celebrity, the Sunday Times sneakingly geared itself up to mock praise, referring to Crisp as a "quasi-transvestite homosexual." The Washington Post, however, called him, "an international treasure".

He has played Queen Elizabeth I in a Hollywood movie; appeared in Philadelphia with Oscar-winning Tom Hanks; made a pop video with Boy George; and portrayed Wilde's Lady Bracknell in a Broadway production of The Importance of Being Earnest.

Quentin Crisp notes he has never been part of any gay lib movement, never been on a march, and never protested. Nor has he ever had a long-standing relationship.

He says he had his own moral code: "I know that sounds a bit priggish. I made my own rules – and I did have some.

"I couldn't live with anybody. I like living alone. This is my kingdom, and I can do as I like in it. At last, after 70 years of being no more than himself, Quentin Crisp seems truly fulfilled: "I have two or three days a week when I just loll around the room in a filthy dressing gown and do nothing. On others, I'll doll myself up and go out.

"There are always crazes in New York. But I ignore all those things like 'don't go down there… that's a bad street'. Shortly, I shall be going out again," he informs me.

"But I shall ignore the Millennium, except that it will be an excuse for a street party. Everyone will scream and shout, but I shall hide in my room.

"I shall mostly hide for my birthday. Last year I was in the theatre, so I worked on Christmas Day."

Tomorrow, Quentin Crisp flies to England: "I believe there are seats and tables on the pavements and people talking, smiling, laughing and waving to one another. Things unknown in my time there."

And now, he will be in Liverpool: "It's not really a performance. I go on stage and tell people how to be happy.

"I have only ever had about half a dozen questions calculated to embarrass me, I treat them with the contempt they deserve."

Quentin Crsip born Dec 25, 1908, died Nov 21, 1999.

A MERSEY POET ON HIS RHYME AND REASON

Brian Patten
Poet

March, 2000

Brian Patten, one of the famed Mersey poets of the 60s, went on to become the UK's best-selling author of children's verse. Forty years on, the Wavertree-born bard has swapped the banks of the Mersey for those of a Devonshire river.

BUT now he's heading home once more – to launch his latest poetry book for kids at the Everyman Theatre.

In the heady days when Liverpool became world capital of popular culture, there might have been John, Paul, George and Ringo at the Cavern.

But there was also Roger, Adrian and Brian at Streates, a coffee bar in Mount Pleasant.

Roger McGough, Adrian Henri and Brian Patten – for some reason always listed in that order – were the almost-as-famous Liverpool 8 Poets (nobody talked of Toxteth then).

Yet, ironically, it was Brian, at just 15 years of age, who first published the poems of McGough and Henri, both more than 10 years his senior.

Bob Wooler, the Cavern DJ, had tried to persuade Brian to

become a pop singer.

"Although I went to the Cavern, I was not really a manic music fan," recalls Brian.

"Instead, I ran a literary magazine called Underdog. It started off duplicated, and ended up printed."

The circulation rose to 2,500, and also featured poems by the American mentor of Bob Dylan, Allen Ginsberg.

"Alllen was an open and charismatic person, so people were open with him," says Brian.

The first of Brian's own public words were in the Bootle Times, where he worked as a reporter.

"I went for a job in a butchers," he says. "I didn't get it, but his cousin worked on the newspaper, so I went there. Now you couldn't do that nowadays – could you?

"My first byline was on a story about a girl with a hole in the heart. Human interest, I think you still call it."

But, at 17, Brian's interest in journalism waned: "Sitting on the station platform waiting to go to work in a suit – hot and sweaty – wasn't my scene."

Instead he sold papers at the Pier Head and cut the grass in Sefton Park.

At night, McGough, Henri and Patten would read their work to the coffee bar punters.

"We were performance poets before the phrase was invented," he says. "The delivery was as important as the writing. The idea of being able to give poetry back to the people."

One of the poets Brian worked with was the tragic Stevie Smith.

"You don't know they are going to be legends one day," he says.

"Stevie was a tiny, sharp tongued woman. Quite wonderful really. She was looked down on by lots of establishment poets at the time, because they thought what she was writing was doggerel, it was so off the wall."

But everything seemed up for rediscovery in the 60s.

The Liverpool poets' early streetwise work, says Brian, "was the opposite of what was going on at the university at the time – a very narrow outlook."

Their joint anthology became the best-selling poetry book of all time, clearing more than a million copies to date.

For years, they travelled as a trio and, even when Roger and Brian moved to London, there were occasional reunion dates. They had been planning a show in Italy, just before Adrian Henri suffered a life threatening stroke last year.

By the 80s, Brian, with the 120,000-sale slim volume Gargling With Jelly, had become the UK's top-selling children's poet.

That success continues with translations into Spanish, German and Polish.

Now 54, he has a new tome for youngsters out next week, Juggling With Gerbils. "I've never worked out how I write it. We must never forget how intensely children feel things.

"I like writing for kids. It's giving yourself permission to play with words again, and poetry is much more popular in schools now. It's a different kind of poetry that never used to exist."

Another recent collection, Armada is dedicated to the memory of Brian's mother, Stella, who raised him in '50s Wavertree, and died five years ago.

"She was very proud of my poems," he says. "She used to put my books on the mantelpiece like birthday cards and dust them. But she never read the grown-up poems, only the children's stuff."

Today, Brian's grown-up poems are analysed by scholars, studied in schools, and read at memorial services.

"I'm flattered. In times of grief, people do turn to poetry," he says.

Particularly apt is a verse called How Long Is A Man's Life? "It's not a God poem," notes Brian. "But I think it's used because it sounds religious without being so."

Brian attended the now disappeared Sefton Park Secondary Modern School, being promoted from C to A stream after the headmaster read one of his essays.

He recalls: "There was one particular teacher, a Mr Sutcliffe, who was obsessed by opera, so he would always tell us the plots. Wonderful stories, like The Flying Dutchman."

But it was a Liverpool Echo report about a leprechaun being spotted in Jubilee Park, Kensington, during the summer of '64, that inspired an early book called The Moon's Last Case.

And there was later a play called The Pig And The Junkie, written for the Everyman.

He even recorded an LP of Aesop's Fables with Cleo Laine.

But the first stirring of Brian's creative imagination came from Liverpool street singers: "I've still got the image in my head," says Brian.

"Lots of sea shanties. These were men who seemed to me then to be old. But they were actually young men who had come home, crippled and blighted by war."

Despite success, Brian has not collected any academic medals. There have been no honorary doctorates.

"I think I've been too much of a naughty boy over the years," he says with a grin.

"But I've no big ambition. If I went away tomorrow and was never heard of again, that would be fine by me."

After the tour to promote his new books – at major festivals, theatres and conferences in big towns and cities – Brian will go to his home in the West Country and, hopefully, just sit and write.

"Then there are long periods of time when I am not writing anything, which is depressing," he adds.

And he has a confession to make: "I feel I've become terribly unfaithful to the River Mersey.

"The river I have a love affair with now is the Dart, in Devon. I've never learned to drive, so have a small boat I use to go shopping. I go down to Dartmouth and get provisions that way. Water is my main source of inspiration. Always water.

"Armada is a book about Liverpool. The themes of the docks and the river flow though it quite a lot. But, unless you knew the place, you wouldn't see that."

Brian Patten, poet , born Liverpool, February 7, 1946.

TO RUSSIA WITH LOVE ... FRANKLY SPEAKING

Frank Clarke
Writer

November, 1984

I want to be rich... by the way, I'm a socialist," says Frank Clarke, indulging himself in a little of the old Jekyll and Hyde.

WE'RE talking movies anyway. About the start of a new film industry... in Liverpool.

And why not?

"Instead of all the talent lying down in London, why shouldn't they come here?" asks Frank. It seems logical enough.

The 29-year old Kirkbyite is a creator of what's billed as the first feature film to be made in Liverpool by Liverpool people.

It's called Letter To Brezhnev and for the next three weeks the camera crew and actors will be whizzing around town putting it all together in predictable places like clubs and pubs and on the ferry, and less well-known locations like the ladies loo of the Odeon.

Are they flushed with success? Well not yet. It's a big gamble. The big test will come when they try to sell it on the commercial cinema circuit.

The good news so far is that it's got the backing of folk like

Willy Russell and his wife. Anne. He's making his film acting debut playing a reporter on the sniff for a story. She is acting as a producer for the film company set up to handle it –, Pleasure Pictures.

All they have is a room in the Everyman Theatre annexe and a budget of around £200,000 – piffling by usual filming standards.

One of the 'imported' stars, Peter Firth has just been working on a movie about vampires in outer space, with a 30 million dollar back-up. So there's your comparison.

There are some anonymous angels 'putting up cash – a gent from the Isle of Man has put in £20,000 and personally offered to act as driver for the crew. But more than half the money is being found by the team themselves in the hope of a good sales return.

In the meantime, everyone's living on pauper's expenses.

Frank's storyline is about two Kirkby scallies, Elaine and Teresa, who meet up with a couple of Russians sailors during a night on the town. But the ship is leaving port the next day, so Elaine decides to write to Mr. B at the Kremlin.

"It's not politics in the usual sense," says Frank. It's about the politics of love. People tend to forget that the folk in Kirkby do actually fall in love. . ."

Playing one of the girl's is Frank's sister, Margi Clarke, better known, perhaps , as Margox from her Granada days.

And despite the title, which came from one of Margi's songs, the story is set in the present. "I was going to call it Galtieri's Note," says Frank, "but somehow that doesn't sound right."

The script, now in its fifth draft, has been the lynch-pin of Clarke's creative work to date.

It got him work as a Brookside writer, churning out 14

episodes before he decided it was "just a formula, too much like a factory."

Then the play version, performed at the Unity Theatre for a week, was seen by Willy and Anne Russell on the final night.

Russell, not one to bandy about praise, has since gone on record describing Clarke as "a truly talented writer, revelling in language."

And it was Russell who put his money where his mouth was, and gave Frank Clarke £200 and a typewriter, just when it seemed that his film hopes were grounded.

"I was on my uppers. The electric was about to be cut off."

Before the change of fortunes, Frank says that he had been "a professional scally and a professional guest."

There had been the odd foray into the theatre. With his mate Chris Bernard (who's directing Brezhnev) he'd put on a show at the Playhouse called Dr.White and the Lilletes. One performance ended with a frisky feminist pouring a pint of lager over his head.

Frank Clarke has never been compromised over his art, which is one thing that delights him about Brezhnev. There's no big distributor putting an oar in, as happened when they wanted Dolly Parton instead of Julie Walters for Russell's Educating Rita.

Letter to Brezhnev will remain raw, funny and true to life. Even though a scene in which girls mention masturbation may have cost them a county council grant.

"The Labour Party have no sense of humour and never have had," says Frank.

One other hiccup has been the refusal of permission to film

at Liverpool airport. So they're using Manchester instead.

But other folk have chipped in: Lewis's with £700 worth of costumes, the Atlantic Tower Hotel with the free use of their penthouse suite. It all adds up to a feeling of optimism for the future.

"Yes it might have been the beginning of a film industry in Liverpool," says Annie Russell. "Certainly, Willy would be interested in writing something himself if this project works."

Frank Clarke, writer, born Liverpool 1955.

DAME FOR A LAUGH!

Dame Edna
Housewife Superstar

November, 1995

My favourite celebrity in whatever guise...

"IS that a moving picture you're taking?"Dame Edna asks the Liverpool Echo photographer. To dignify the occasion,the Australian housewife superstar clouts another member of the paparazzi with gladdies.

"The Dame – by her own estimation the most popular and gifted woman in the world today – walks the full length of the red carpet rolled out in her honour.

An admirer rushes the security cordon with a bunch of flowers: "Oh, those pendulous, pink, nodding stalks," enthuses Dame Edna in appreciation.

Clearly it's been one of those days. The lipstick is slightly smudged and the rings – worn on the outside of her gloves – are twisted.

"As a squillionairness, I don't HAVE to do this," she tells the fans. "But I'm a fun loving person. It's all part of my philosophy of sharing. I was born to share and give myself."

Edna quickly regains her regal self-composure. Like her friend the Queen she never forgets a face: "I remember little old you, darling," she tells me.

"Not as young as you were – and not as thin either. But I mean that in a caring way. I really do."

Away from the adoring crowds, Edna relaxes in a plush hotel suite and fixes me with one of her more telling stares. "I don't think the good people of Liverpool have ever seen an icon before," she confides.

Well they're about to get the chance.

Edna, in company with Australian cultural attache Doctor Sir Leslie Patterson, and their joint manager, Barry Humphries, decamp at the Empire Theatre for a week.

"I do expect very special treatment when I come among you. I want to make it quite clear that I am the acceptable face of Australia. I am not a separatist like the people in Liverpool. "But to start with, I want to give you an exclusive, and make a rather spooky announcement: I was Gracie Fields in another life.

"And it's quite possible that my late husband Norm, was George Formby – although he looked like Arthur Askey."

Despite being pan-global, Dame Edna has many other intimate Liverpool insights and connections. She is convinced for instance, that Maggie May was really Mary Magdalene "who came to Liverpool after our Lord passed away."

But it's not all historical

"A very close friend of mine is little Ringo Starr. He could leave his skis under my bed any day."

With Dame Edna, of course, will be her faithful bridesmaid Madge Allsop. "She will be making a guest appearance, which is an historic first.

"Doctors said I over-excite people, so you'll need Madge to calm you down. But please don't encourage her with laughter and applause.

"She once caught my bouquet across the back of her neck. It wiped out an entire nerve centre."

And what of Sir Les?

Dame Edna's mood darkens: "THAT man! He once took me to the pictures, but did nothing but sneeze. I remember he bought me a box of Black Magic and whispered something pretty unseemly: "Would you like a hard one or a soft one?"

Dame Edna, meanwhile, will be as frank and fearless as ever with her audience: "I may give them a tough time – but they expect it. If only people could see the avalanche of love that comes through my letter box.

"Liverpool people are warm and giving. Not like the south of England. They are cold fish down there. You never hear of ''the well known Kent comedian' or 'the famous Dorset humourist, do you?

"Laughter is wonderful exercise. The aerobics of the soul."

Subjects touched on could include fashion, feminism, womanhood – even sex – although Edna thinks that sex is over-publicised. She considers that grown-up people should be used to it by now.

However, as a mother, she is willing to advertise on childbirth: "Women often try to frighten other women on this. Provided you relax, childbirth should be like popping a champagne cork."

And what about fashion?

"Well I rarely wear a bra," says Dame Edna in a rare moment of self exposure. "I am not big in the bosom department. I could never have been a topless model, although I do have other attributes, such as lovely legs.

"As it happens, I prefer tights to stockings as I travel so much."

Do you ever ladder them?

"Not unless I undress with all my jewellery on." Even after two decades in the international limelight, Edna remains tireless, aware and content.She has, as she points out, succeeded at everything she has put her hand to.

But if she was ever to be honoured by the Queen, what form would it take?

"Well in Australia, I would of course, be Baroness of Moonee Ponds. But , were I British, I could choose the title of Baroness Toxteth."

And now it's time to sample some good old northern cuisine. Dame Edna declines a black pudding "because you don't know what blood group it is but. I do like those butties!" So butties it is... smoked salmon butties, of course.

Born in the Melbourne suburb of Kew, February 2, 1934. Barry Humphries was educated at Melbourne Grammar School and Melbourne University, where he read law, philosophy and fine arts.

PLAY IT AGAIN, MISS BACALL

Lauren Bacall
Sex Siren and Screen Goddess

June, 1985

It was not quite the average day in the hack trade. I could have had lunch with James Bond, but I was not feeling sufficiently high tech to meet 007.

INSTEAD, I decided to drop in on the living legendary Hollywood star with a capital S – Lauren Bacall.

The former Mrs Humphrey Bogart is playing a raddled has-been of an actress in Tennessee Williams' Sweet Bird Of Youth.

It's the flip side of the American dream philosophy, but Ms Bacall has lost none of her razzle.

She sweeps up in a powder–blue Jag and climbs out in a yellow stripey outfit, which gives every impression of a wasp taking leave of a wedding bouquet.

I thought up that little gem of prose before I found out that she really was in stinging mood. Apparently a copy of the Daily Mail had been delivered with her breakfast. She didn't like the bit about still building up her reputation.

"Are you sober now that I've left you for so long?" she asks.

"I put my thrice-filled gin and tonic glass – now empty down on the table and scoop up a salted peanut... this is going to be a hard one to crack.

Ladies first: "I am an actress.

"I am damn tired of being put into categories by the press. I am a professional and have been for 40 years. I am appearing with distinguished actors, and being directed by a great writer (Harold Pinter). And having reached this stage of my life, I feel I can say what I like."

They keep calling me a Hollywood 'quote' star. I mean, I haven't lived there for 25 years. I have been in the theatre steadily since 1966.

"The press keep going on about this ageing film star stuff, as if, after 35, you should cut your throat. I don't understand why people aren't meant to continue to produce in their lives. Especially in England where actors are always respected much more so than in America.

"It's as if they don't understand that people are meant to get better and learn and grow... the attitudes here are becoming more like America."

Well, that seemed to have cleared the air a bit. And blunted my pencil. Oh, for another G and T.

The mood grows softer. It's not me she's getting at you understand. It's just all the legend stuff, which she thought she'd left behind.

The voice is still sultry, so sultry in fact, you wonder why she didn't make all her pictures in asbestos. And she's looking just fine for a lady of 60.

She'd come to talk business, not to play on the mobile altar of halcyon Hollywood.

And yet, she's not daft enough to think that the world doesn't still view her as the girl who became the new Garbo. The girl, who in 1943 was an usherette in a New York theatre, and within 12 months was co-starring with Bogart in To Have and Have Not.

By 1945, she was his 20 year-old-bride.

He always called her Betty or Baby; she called him Bogie - just like everyone else.

The thing is, Bacall in 1985 wants to move on. She will, of course, talk about Bogie – "He was a man of tremendous qualities, he stood for good things.

"His standards were high."

But now, the play's the thing.

Why did she choose a Tennessee Williams play?

"Look, I've only ever done comedy and musicals on stage.

"I did meet Tennessee Williams once. He said he'd like me to do one of his plays and I told him it was one of my dreams. Working with Pinter as a director has been a bonus, too." She describes him as "one of God's gifts."

There's an obvious integrity to her drift. This is a good play, a good part.

Not just something to do. After all, they soon learned on the film lot back in '48 when she refused to go before the cameras in a swimsuit, that she can in no way be compromised.

"I didn't think I was a cheapskate girl." Bacall recalls, mentioning with obvious displeasure the moguls' fascination for shooting semi-nude girls standing on iced cakes, etcetera.

By this time Miss Bacall is well thawed out. The sting has been retracted.

She's done the lot. Her life has not been free of a little rumour running up and down Sunset Boulevard, but that's life.

"Moss Hart said you should shake your life up every seven years or so. I have – and I think I am wonderful to do this."

We've cracked the nut.

She's smiling – and not afraid to be a little self-mocking.

Lauren Bacall, actress, born New York September 16, 1924. Known for her husky voice and sultry looks, she became a fashion icon in the 1940s and has continued acting to the present day. She is perhaps best known for films such as The Big Sleep, Dark Passage as well as a comedienne, as seen in 1953's How To Marry A Millionaire. She also enjoyed success starring in Broadway musicals.

ABOUT THE AUTHOR

Joe Riley
Journalist, Writer

Joe Riley was the youngest arts editor in Britain when appointed to the Liverpool Echo in 1974. He is now the country's senior serving journalist in such a post...

Joe is also the leader (editorial) writer as well as a columnist for the Echo. This year he was short-listed as UK newspaper columnist of the year.

Joe's work has taken him all over the world, including more than 20 foreign tours with the Royal Liverpool Philharmonic Orchestra, with whom he has also appeared as a soloist/narrator.

As the Echo's award-winning film, theatre, music and fine arts chief critic, he has interviewed and reviewed most of the legendary names in the arts and showbusiness.

Joe is a regular broadcaster for BBC radio and television, as well as having a weekly slot on Classic FM .

His largest ever television audience was 60 million for an American coast-to-coast review of the premiere of Paul McCartney's Liverpool Oratorio.

A visiting senior lecturer in journalism to a number British universities and colleges, Joe is the author of four previous books, including another anthology of Echo articles, The Life of

Riley, published by Headland in 2000.

A copy of his history of Liverpool Cathedral was presented to Her Majesty the Queen on the occasion of the completion of the building in October 1978.

Joe is the first journalist in the history of the Liverpool Echo to be awarded an honorary degree for his journalism, being conferred a Fellow of Liverpool John Moores University in 2002.